indGame

indGame

ROD
R GARCIA

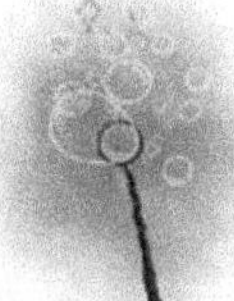

Enchanted Bubble Wand Press

an imprint of

EpiphanyMill Publishing

Text Copyright © 2022 Rod R Garcia

Cover Art Copyright © 2022 Rod R Garcia

Published in the United States by Enchanted Bubble Wand Press, an imprint of EpiphanyMill LLC. Star Valley, AZ

EpiphanyMill Publishing is a registered trademark and the bubble wand colophon is a trademark of EpiphanyMill LLC.

Visit us on the Web! EpiphanyMill.com

Library of Congress Cataloging-in-Publication Data

Garcia, Rod R

IndGame / Rod R Garcia. — First edition.

ISBN 978-1-947691-12-4 (intl. tr. pbk.)

ISBN 978-1-947691-13-1 (eBook)

[1. YA-Fiction. 2. Science-Fiction. 3. Thriller-Fiction.]

I. Title.

Library of Congress Control Number 2022947442

The text of this book is set in 12 Apollo MT Std.

Book design by Rod R Garcia

Edited by E. M. B.

Cover design by Rod R Garcia

Printed in the United States of America

10 9 8 7 6 5 4 3 2 1

First Edition

For Dylan 'Doritos' Dirodis, my friend.

You are missed.

P.S. Packard would appreciate your t-shirt collection

almost as much as me.

SPECIAL THANKS TO:

BETA READERS

Michael Foster

Patrick Matthews

Pat Muxie

Jeremy Lelle

COVER ART CLEANUP

Whendell Souza

COVER ART PHOTOGRAPHY

Betsy Ponce

COVER ART MODEL

Jake Ashton

Video games are bad for you?

That's what they said about Rock 'n' Roll.

~ Shigeru Miyamoto

Prologue

"Take one. indGame commercial. Mic live in three... two... one..."

Exciting electronic music begins to play. It sounds like the '80s are getting a second wind.

~

Welcome to indGame!

Welcome to a future without boundaries!

Have you ever wanted to scale Mount Everest? Maybe your secret dream has always been to explore the Mariana Trench. Or perhaps a game of hopscotch on the dark side of the moon would be more your speed.

Tired of your day job? How does facing down gladiators in an alien arena sound to you? Not really your thing? There's always a need for a new U.S. Marshal in the Arizona boomtown of

Rotgut. Then again, there are always vampires, aliens, and feral humans to take down if you just want to save the world, or nearly indestructible battle suits, if your goal is to enslave it.

Greetings! My name is Hal Campbell, CEO of the indGame Corporation. You can see my son Packard over there, testing out our latest simulator, *Marshal Blood*. He'd wave if he knew he was on camera. Right now, though, he's lost in another world, hot on the trail of a ruthless band of train robbers. He might even catch 'em if the locals don't scalp him first!

You see, using our patented cerebral scanner, coupled with our quantum universal anamnesis database, Q.U.A.D for short, we can import your very essence into our servers. We record your memories, emotions, fears – everything that makes you who you are – to create an in-game character with your precise personality, right down to ticks, twitches, and nasty habits. For all intents and purposes, the character in the game believes itself to be you.

All you need to do is jack into the game and immerse yourself in an experience that's part simulator, part interactive play, and, as far as your brain will be concerned, 100% real.

The best part is, you'll return to the real world without a scratch, but with real memories of your adventures in cyberspace completely intact, like a dream you actually remember. Or a nightmare if that's your bag.

So, whether you're a n00b or l33t, old or young, ability-challenged or triathlete, indGame has something for everyone.

No joysticks or button-mashing required.

indGame — individual gaming at its finest.

~

"Aaaand cut! Alright, folks, that's a wrap. Nice work, Hal."

LEVEL ONE
MEMORY DUMP

1

Tournament of Warlords

The beast drew back his arm, clenching his broad, blood-encrusted fist so tightly, it shook like a centenarian with a bad case of the tremors. Sharp, bony protrusions appearing to serve as knuckles popped audibly, and I braced myself for the next blow.

The crowd roared as I raised my arms in a defensive move, activating a plasma shield that ran between ceramic nodes permanently implanted in my forearms. With my fists balled, and my arms in close enough proximity to one another, the nodes filled the gap with a near-impenetrable energy field that would last as long as I maintained my position.

I braced myself. The view through the energy field was like wearing blue aviator sunglasses. Light filtered through in a cool haze. The beast swung, striking the makeshift shield with the force of a freight train. Bone chips and sparks flew in all directions. A shockwave rippled across the energy field, causing parts of its surface to change momentarily from blue to a shade of violet, a clear sign the barrier had almost been compromised. I winced as the impact jarred the nodes, resonating all the way down to the anchor points in my bones. Immediately, thousands of nanops went to work on the resulting hairline fractures. Within mere seconds, the anchor points were as good as new.

A second blow came just as the nanops finished their task, almost dislodging one of the nodes completely, sending the tiny medical technicians back to work. It appeared their day was just getting started.

The shield's surface became darker. My pain threshold was exploring a new definition for the word 'excruciating', but I held my ground like a retiree with coupons at the cash register.

A third, well-placed strike changed that.

I cried out involuntarily as the powerful fist finally crashed through the barrier, ripping most of the nodes from my bones, leaving them dangling loosely from the flesh of my already battered forearms. The fist connected with my face, smashing my nose and shredding my lips. Teeth flew to the back of my throat, making me gag as the beast's other hand wrapped tightly around my throat, cutting off my air supply.

The beast, known on his home planet as L'OthruC'ant, was an arthrolopithicus. Like many desert-dwelling predatory species, he wore his skeleton on the outside. Virtually covered in bioresponsive armor and possessing unparalleled strength, he was insanely difficult to kill. Yet, with a face resembling a spoiled package of ground beef, and my primary defenses equally disposed, I still wasn't ready to throw in the towel.

L'OthruC'ant noticed as I brought my right knee up between us. I half expected him to react, but his arrogant expression said everything. In his eyes, he had already won. He would let me suffer the pain of a broken knee as a final indignity.

I knew I had precious little time before the arthrolopithicoid ended the fight. *All* fights in the Multiversal Tournament of Warlords ended with at least one fatality.

"Finish it! Finish it! Finish it!" The chant had become the crowd's mantra, and L'OthruC'ant drank it like grape Kool-Aid from a golden chalice. Intoxicated by it and the smell of my blood, he thrust a gore-covered celebratory fist into the air. The crowd stood and showed its approval with a unified roar.

L'OthruC'ant's moment of self-indulgent glory became my window of opportunity. I brought my knee up to my adversary's groin and clenched my foot and toes tightly. A tiny laser implanted in my patella, with a beam like a surgeon's scalpel, bored a needle-sized hole through my flesh and began to work on my opponent's exoskeleton.

Before L'OthruC'ant understood what was happening, the laser simultaneously bisected and cauterized his internal organs. He pulled back slightly, his expression betrayed both surprise and pain. It was in that moment of confusion that I raised my arms into my trademark defensive position. The nanops were fast, but I was by no means healed. I could only hope they'd done enough as I positioned my forearms on either side of L'OthruC'ant's head and clenched my fists tightly.

The field flickered for a moment, but the nanops were responsive and practical in their repair patterns. I was in battle mode, so weapons ops took priority over all else. One final adjustment to the last node in the firing order and the shield sparked to life.

The top of L'OthruC'ant's head slid along the thin layer of energy and landed with a wet thud in the dirt behind me.

The shield sputtered and failed, peppering me with the charred remains of my foe's blood and brains. L'OthruC'ant's body quivered slightly before collapsing on me.

The crowd fell silent as their champion dropped, burying me under his massive frame.

The audience cheered once again as L'OthruC'ant began to move, pleased to see the fight continue. They paused for the briefest of moments, though, as L'OthruC'ant rolled off to the side, and I staggered to my feet. The roar resumed, however, when I boldly raised one bloody fist victoriously into the air.

They had a new champion to cheer for.

Packard Campbell. Remember that name, folks.

2

Packard Campbell

Like I said, my name's Packard Campbell. Most people just call me Pack, except my dad, but I don't mind Packard. So many people stress about how their birth name sounds. Rodneys become Rod, Jakobs become Jake, Richards become Dick. You know what I'm talking about. And why? Because it sounds more mature? Because it rolls off the tongue more easily? Whatever. My name is my name, and I'm proud of it.

Anyway, my name isn't problem. It's everything else.

It's weird. I mostly know who I am, but it's like I've got memories of past lives, or I see glimpses of alternate versions of myself somewhere in the multiverse. It makes zero sense, right? Especially since I think I know where all these memories came from. I beta-test new first-person neural-interface games for my dad's company, indGame. Funny, back to the name thing again. The real name of the company is Individual Gaming, but he calls it indGame. That doesn't sound more mature to me. If you ask me, indGame sounds better as a video game or movie title. Check us out at IndividualGaming.com if you're interested. I've got my own profile and everything. Take that, Vic E. Parker! Oh, sorry. Vic was my middle school bully. I occasionally need to remind the universe I'm not the slaghead he always made me out to be. It's cathartic. I'll get over it one day, you'll see.

Oh, dang, I squirreled, didn't I? Where was I? Richard becomes Dick... Oh, yeah, beta-testing. I'm the primary tester for all the new games that indGame releases. You've probably played at least a few of them: *Tournament of Warlords*, *Marshal Blood*, *Gifted*, *Animehem*, and *String Theories* are all currently available. I've tested more than twenty others that haven't even been released yet. I think *Tom Mux: Space Marine* was my favorite, but *LepreKong* was a flippin' trip, and I actually peed a little while playing dad's latest cosmic horror game, *Crawlspace*.

Hey, don't laugh. I pee a little during lots of the games. I don't even have to be afraid or excited. See, when I was in middle school, doctors diagnosed me with a previously undiscovered neuromuscular disorder, Atrophic Lamin A Sclerosis, that's been slowly but surely eating away at my ability to use my own body. I call it ALAS, since it's like Progeria and Lou Gehrig's disease had a really colicky baby, then put energy drinks in its bottle. Yeah, I joke, but it sucks. The first symptoms reared their ugly head during my freshman year in high school. By the time I was a junior, I was completely numb from the belly button down. At least Vic never saw me like this. Slaghead would have been a compliment compared to the bullshit comments I would've had to endure as my body forgot how to walk. I'm mostly glad mom didn't have to watch dad and me go through this. She died when I was nine. The doctors think her condition and mine might be related, but they can't be completely sure. She was wonderful and I miss her every day. Dad does too, but he's strong in ways I don't think she could have been. If she hadn't died, watching me die would have killed her anyway. Oh, yeah, I'm dying too. I've got three to five years tops before my body won't breathe on its own. I told dad that I don't want to end up a vegetable kept alive by machines. Even though I know it hurts him, I'm old enough to request a do not resuscitate order.

Crap, I squirreled again. Sorry. Rodney, beta testing? Peeing myself, that's it. I've played all of dad's games from start to finish and found all the gold star items and platinum levels to boot. I'm proud of that accomplishment, to be honest.

Okay, so this is where it gets weird. My consciousness gets cloned into the system when I jack in, so the games play like I'm actually the character, leaving memories of the game in my head that feel as real as, well, reality. I've always been able to solidly distinguish between reality and the virtual world. Today, though, things are different. Jumbled memories keep coming at me rapid-fire. One moment, I'm remembering an Easter egg hunt with my mom. The next, I'm reliving slicing the top of some alien warlord's head off in a multiversal coliseum. I'm on the verge of my first panic attack in half a decade, and the floodgates don't seem to be planning to close anytime soon.

Whisper. I remember. *Whisper...*

Hold onto your horses, folks. Here we go again...

3

Marshal Blood

My horse shuddered nervously as I guided her into the narrow passageway between the boulders. "Easy girl," I whispered, stroking her mane gently. "We're okay." I was lying of course. Whisper knew my vocal tones as well as the flies that followed us knew the reach of her tail.

I knew the canyon that lay ahead of us was a deathtrap, plain and simple. Between the bloodthirsty savages still calling the territory home, and the murderous train robbers I was trailing, and were almost certainly lying in wait for me in the narrow expanse ahead, I'd be lucky to make it out alive.

I'd never been one to be frightened off by a little danger, and I had the scars to prove it. As lawmen went, my quarry knew there were three possible outcomes once Packard Campbell, known in lawful circles as Marshal Blood, and amongst lowlife varmints as

The Bloodhound, was on their scent. One, you ended up in jail, two, you ended up dead, or three, I ended up dead. It was usually number two. Seeing as I was still kicking up dust and bringing ne'er-do-wells to justice, option three had never played out. I'd been close, but close didn't offer up very favorable odds to those on the wrong side of the law.

"Woah girl."

I drew back on the reins, though Whisper had already stopped. She knew my body language, after all. She snorted nervously, clearing her sinuses, and took a whiff of the scent on the wind.

Gun oil. Fresh. I smelled it too. It traveled the breeze accompanied by the faint aromas of gunpowder, chewin' tobacco, and sweat.

~

I dismounted and tied the reins to a loose branch of scrub brush jutting out from the wall next to us. I crept away from Whisper, who remained as silent as the eye of a storm, and ducked into a crevasse large enough to shield me from three of four sides. Digging a small, cracked mirror from my vest pocket, I scanned the narrow passage around me.

The Lubbock Gang consisted of six men: three brothers, two lifelong friends, and a well-paid hired gun. The odds of them scattering like exposed cellar rats at the first sign of danger were slim to none.

I spotted the first two men quickly. The hired gun, a former Confederate soldier turned mercenary known only as Bly, perched about twenty feet ahead and thirty feet up, at the top of the canyon wall. Bly carried a Marlin 1893 lever-action 30-30 and wore his pistol slung low on his right thigh. The butt of the gun faced forward so he could cross-draw with his left hand. He was at close enough range to put a hole in me the size and relative messiness of a whorehouse spittoon. Bly crouched behind a sizable

boulder, perfectly shielding him from the canyon's point of entry,

though from my vantage point, he was nothing more than a sitting

duck in an old, tan leather duster.

Closest to Bly was Garrett Long; one dangerous third of the

murderous Long brothers. The Long brothers were inseparable

and had a strict fraternal code of honor that bound them more

tightly than blood-brothers, making them some of the most feared

and unpredictable outlaws to ever ride the range. He was stretched

out on his belly roughly ten feet from Bly, resembling a huge

rattlesnake casually sunning itself in the desert heat. Garrett also

carried a rifle, bolt-action, though I couldn't determine the make

from his hidden position. I like to know as much as possible about

my quarry before heading into a firefight, including what kind of

guns they're packing. In the right hands, a firearm is nothing less

than a physical extension of the wielder. Just like a boxer needs to know if their opponent is a right-hander or a southpaw, I need to know what manner of gun a man is holding.

It took another minute or so to find the other two Long brothers, Hank and Bobby, and one of the two friends who completed the gang. Black Burt was as pale a sumbitch as ever crawled out from underneath a rock, but he was a deadeye with a revolver, and one of the most notorious gunfighters west of the ol' Mississippi. I couldn't see the second friend, a wily Irish varmint simply named Red, anywhere, though it was unlikely he was far. These men were as thick as thieves. Maybe that's a redundant analogy, seeing as they were thieves, but hey, if the boot fits, right?

Hank and Bobby each carried a Winchester shotgun. Hank's was an 1887 and Bobby's was a 1901. They also had single sidearms slung low on their right thighs, butt facing back, gunfighter style. Burt loosely gripped twin 1860 Colt revolvers, and occasionally tipped them back as if he was silently firing at an unseen target.

Hank, Bobby, and Burt had taken up defensive positions in locations where they wouldn't risk catching each other, or Garret and Bly, in a crossfire.

I studied them for a moment, doing the math in my head. If they were avoiding a crossfire, that only left two places for Red to hide. Red would either be directly at the entrance to the canyon, which I knew wasn't right, because I'd already have a bullet in my brainpan from the ride in.

The other location was-

A revolver's hammer cocked less than three inches from the back of my head.

~

"Easy there, Red," I said quietly. "You should be awfully damned proud of yourself. Nobody ever got the drop on me this close or this quietly. You sure you ain't one of them Kung Fu masters or somethin?"

Red snickered at the comment. "Yer a funny man, Mr. Bludhoond. It's a pity I'm gonna havta kill ya now. Ye might've had quite the career on Vaudeville."

Red's reputation preceded him, and I was quite sure it would be the only thing that might save my life. "Come on now, Red. You know you've never shot a man in the back. That Irish honor, or some bullshit like that. I understand you like to look a man in the eye before you kill him."

Red breathed out through his nose, sounding like Whisper when she sensed a trap. "I might say t'the Devil with honor, jest this once. It would be worth it t'be able t'say I was the man t'finally take doon the Bludhoond. Doncha fancy?"

"Maybe," I conceded, realizing I could see his gun barrel in the old mirror I still held between my fingers. Christ, but that guy had steady hands. "If you think you could live with yourself, and your secret, shameful, dishonorable deed. Just imagine what your Pa would think. His own *boyo* couldn't face me like a man, so he shot me in the back. Go ahead, lad. I'll tell your old man about it when I see him in Hell."

"Blast ye and yer sheep-shite yammerin'!" Red fumed. For the barest of moments, his focus wavered, and his gun sight strayed to the left. It only moved by a hair, but it would have to be enough.

I compensated for Red's twitch by quickly rolling to the right. I ended up on my back, face to face with the man who, allegedly, would only shoot a man if he could see his eyes. His eyes were narrowed, partly because he directly faced the mid-morning sun, but mostly because I'd pissed him off, *royally*.

"Damn you," he shouted, as he overcorrected and tugged off a shot that slammed into the soil just to the right of my head.

As Red palmed the revolver's hammer back, I brought my right boot up as hard as I was able to from my prone position and drove the pointed tip right up between his bowed legs.

Red squealed like a stuck pig as he squeezed off a final shot. The left side of my face felt like someone pressed an icicle against it. I knew I'd been hit, though how badly remained in question.

The mirror in my left hand broke off where the old crack had been. As Red doubled over me in pain, I lashed out with the remaining shard, and brought it across Red's exposed throat. The wound was shallow, there was no spray of blood or anything quite so dramatic, but it was clearly painful enough that Red's left hand reflexively shot from his aching crotch and pressed against his throat. His eyes bugged as he felt a warm trickle of blood seep between his fingers. I'm sure the blood felt like a lot more than it really was. Honestly, Red might've lived if not for the bullet I put between his eyes in the second that followed. The fingers on his right hand flew open in surprise and his revolver dropped, clattering down the incline, and landing somewhere in the rocks below.

I leapt to my feet and shoved Red backwards before he could land on me like a stinky old sack of onions. His body tumbled down the embankment to join his fallen revolver.

Shouts sounded from below, but there was no sign of movement. The others were trying to determine who was down — one of them, or dare they believe, me.

I didn't give them the chance to figure it out. As the remaining bandits shouted out to each other in frustrated confusion, I pulled my trusty Henry from my rifle-scabbard on my back and began to fire.

As I said before, in the right hands, a firearm is nothing less than a physical extension of the wielder. When I'm firing my weapons, there's no saying where my hands end, and my guns begin. Finger and trigger become one, and the rifle butt knows my shoulder like a baby knows the warm embrace of its mother's arms. My eyes are autotuned to the sights of my rifle and my pistol, and when it comes to my trusty ol' shotgun, no sighting is necessary, my friend. I can dead-eye a target as easily as pointing a finger.

Burt was the first to fall. A hole appeared in his forehead as I squeezed off a round, and he slumped to the hardpan soil without any fanfare, his twin Colts splayed out in different directions like abstract art.

I took out Hank and Bobby much the same way. Hank took a slug to the temple. Bobby, flinching as Hank's head jerked back, took one to the throat. Hank never even knew he'd been hit, but Bobby took a minute or so to die. The desperado fired off a last wild shot that clipped an unsuspecting cactus as he choked on blood, bile, and chewin' tobacco.

Once I was satisfied Bobby was beyond chambering another round, I let my focus shift down to Garrett and Bly. Garret leapt to his feet as he realized one or both of his brothers were down. He scrambled ahead like a well-armed hermit crab, shouting my name like a nun scolding an ill-behaved student. Bly clearly knew where I was. He wisely allowed the frantic Garrett to stay between us, using him as a moving meat-shield. I chambered another round and fired at Garrett, striking him in the shoulder. I was already chambering again when Garrett's uncoordinated run slowed to an even less coordinated stumble. He threw his head back in surprise and agony. I was shocked to see an arrowhead protruding from his Adam's apple like a kebab.

Bly, realizing the arrow'd been fired from the rear of his supposedly safe position, rolled forward in an awkward somersault, and began to zigzag in my direction. Apparently, he preferred incarceration to death. A small hatchet adorned with beads and feathers whizzed past his head, ending up lodged in yet another unfortunate cactus.

Arrows zinged dangerously close to Bly, one clipping his boot heel as he hot footed it for my narrow alcove in the rocks. I felt a little better knowing none of the arrows or tomahawks were coming from behind me, but I was also well aware that if Red could get the drop on me, then so could the locals.

My beef wasn't with the natives, but when an arrow put a hole in my favorite canteen, I realized they were out for blood, plain and simple. Bly's blood, my blood, if we didn't belong on their land, we were fair game. Whisper was safe, of course. The locals didn't scalp horses. They'd take her back and feed her apples and turnips while they brushed her. At least there was that.

Bly made it to me faster than a rabbit bein' chased by a hawk. Just like that, I was sardined into a stone crevice with one of the most dangerous men west of the Pecos. Strange bedfellows, as the old man said.

"Seems ma meal ticket's dead," Bly wheezed. His loose drawl betrayed a distinctly southern upbringing. "If'n ye don't mind, I'd rather take ma chances coverin' yer back, since I'm right sure yer lawman's code says ye got to cover mine."

I nodded curtly. "You do realize, if we get outta this alive, I'm gonna hav'ta take you in, son."

Bly smirked. "If'n we do get outta this alive, Marshal, ye can try to take me in. Ye have ma word as a commanding officer of the Confederate States of America on that."

I laughed as a pair of arrows thunked into the rocks to my left. "The South lost, son."

Bly drew his pistol and aimed it towards where the arrows seemed to be coming from. "The South will rise again, Marshal. Ye can count on me as much as ye can count on that."

Well, I thought, *that's not encouraging at all.*

~

Arrows continued to rain down on the stone notch where Bly and I hid. I noticed their accuracy increased with each incoming wave. As the locals got closer, their line of sight got wider. At least we could count on being able to see them as soon as they could see us. I made sure all my guns were fully loaded and ready to fire as soon as the whites of black greasepaint-covered eyes came into view. My Henry repeater, a marvel of modern weaponry that held sixteen rounds in the clip and could fire up to twenty-eight of those bad boys per minute, was up and at the ready. A scout or two would likely come ahead of the actual hunting party, and my rifle would be just the thing to pick 'em off before they could fire an arrow at either Bly or me. My shotgun leaned against my elbow. It would be more useful when the group got closer together. Like the Henry, I could get off several shots in a short period of time. As a last resort, I could quickdraw my revolver like Zeus tossing lightning bolts, but the revolver was the least accurate of the three. As fast as our stalkers were known to be, accuracy was the most likely thing to get us out of our current predicament.

When I say predicament, please understand, I've been in worse situations before, but not many. It was the first time I'd found myself partially relying on the likes of Bly for my survival. I trusted my skin to nobody but myself, and maybe the local sheriff, Clem Pickett. Clem was a loyal lawman, though far too chauvinistic to make a smooth transition into the approaching twentieth century. He held some antiquated and downright offensive viewpoints on women, people of any other color, and folks subscribing to lifestyles or ideas contrary to his own. Clem Pickett was lily-white and as conservative as a preacher collecting the Sunday morning tithe. But as much as you'd never find me at a cookout with the gun-totin' Neanderthal, I'd prefer his gun at my side than this Confederate, lowlife sellout. I guess beggars can't be choosers, though, can we?

"Marshall," Bly said in the loudest whisper he could muster. "If'n ye call out to that horse ye got tied yonder, it'll come a runnin' up the hill, and provide the cover we'd need to get free of this-here deathtrap!"

"Of all the lily-livered, cowardly things to suggest." I glared at him, considering ending our uneasy partnership with a bullet right then and there.

"Or not," he said reassuringly, tipping his head sheepishly, and raising a scar-split eyebrow. The scar ran from somewhere under his hairline, and all the way down his cheek to his jawline. It barely nicked his eyelid, and looked like it hurt like a motherf-

"Jesus!" Bly hissed. My eyes followed his sudden shift in attention. An arrow stuck out of his right shoulder. The arrowhead protruded out the other side ever so slightly. The outlaw pursed his lips over gritted teeth and breathed sharply through his nose. "Lucky fer us, I'm a leftie," he said finally. "Is it clean through?"

"Mostly," I replied quietly. "But we're gonna need to get it out after we get clear of the locals. They're close. Otherwise, that shot never would've got so deep."

Bly nodded. His eyes blazed with determination and beads of sweat peppered his windburned brow. He was a survivor. The South might not be returning, but when it came to sheer skills as a gunfighter, I had to admit, there were certainly worse men to be stuck with.

I reached out, and without giving him any warning, I snapped the arrow off an inch or so from the entry wound. Bly's teeth remained gritted, but his lips parted like the Red Sea. As he quietly exhaled, I heard the faintest hint of a growl. Then, without a word, Bly sealed his lips and nodded again, breathing hard through his nose. I tossed the arrow aside, and the first of the natives leapt into view.

I can't rightly say who fired the shot that killed him. Bly and I pulled our triggers almost simultaneously. There was only evidence of one bullet hole in his chest as the warrior slammed lifelessly into the rocks in his path.

And that started it.

From the first of the warriors to the last, we dropped more than thirty men. It wasn't satisfying or glorious. It was survival. Without a second thought, we killed every man who came at us. When the dust settled, the only sounds remaining were dripping blood, Bly's heavy breathing, and a quick, approving whinny from Whisper.

I picked up one of the feather-adorned hatchets and Bly put his hand on my wrist. I looked at him and let his eyes follow mine down to his wounded shoulder. He looked back at me, understanding my intent, and released my wrist.

"Brace yourself," I warned. I placed the flat side of the hatchet's blade against the broken end of the arrow and pushed.

Bly finally cried out as the arrowhead finished its trip through his flesh and ended up poking all the way out. Stepping behind him, I placed a notch in the edge of the hatchet over the shaft of the arrow, securing the weapon like a handle behind the arrowhead. I pulled for all I was worth, and the remaining third of the arrow came out as smoothly as a knife through butter. I stumbled backwards clumsily as it pulled out, and Bly took the opportunity to be the varmint I knew him to be. Taking advantage of my brief distraction, he picked up my Colt SAA from where I'd set it on the rocks to his left and shoved the barrel right in my face.

~

"Gotta say, lawman. Yer as good as the stories make ye out t'be." Bly looked conflicted, clearly caught somewhere between admiration and wanting to get his ass to freedom. "If'n I thought there was even the slightest chance ye'd let me go, I wouldn't be doing this."

"You know I cain't do that, Bly," I said. "I cain't break the law, even outta gratitude."

Bly nodded. He didn't look any happier than I felt killing the natives. "Then I cain't let ye live, Marshal," he conceded. "I will take right good care of yer horse and guns, though."

"Well, isn't that kind of you," I asked. "Do me a favor and make it a clean shot, will ya'? Forehead, not face."

Bly nodded amicably. "A'yup. Seems the least I kin do." He looked at my Colt like a man inspecting a horse before purchasing it. "Fine weapon, Marshal. Looks like ye maintained it well. I promise I'll keep up the tradition. By the way, thank ye kindly fer leaving a bullet chambered. I was counting as ye fired at the end of the firefight. Turns out, ye only needed five of yer six rounds."

"You were countin', eh? That's right trig of you." I shuffled my feet a bit. "Mind if I ask one more favor, Bly?"

"Aw, hell, I'm feelin' generous t'day." Bly grinned. I saw he was missing more than a few of his front teeth. "What else ye want from ol' Bly, son?"

"When you tell the story about how you did the old Bloodhound in, leave me a shred of dignity, will ya'?"

Bly laughed at that. "Ha! Sure, lawman. As much dignity as a man who died disarmed and horseless deserves. Now put up yer damned chin so's I kin git on with ma day!"

I put up my chin bravely. As he pressed the barrel to my forehead, I asked, "You know what the only problem with that Colt is, Bly?"

"I guess I'll have t'find out on ma own now, won't I," Bly said as he pulled the trigger.

~

Click.

The worst sound anyone can hear when they're relying on the gun in their hand.

"That," I said, as I dropped to my knees and put the hatchet through the front of Bly's boot.

"Jesus!" Bly cried out, dropping the Colt to the hardpan soil. "What did ye…" He trailed off and dropped to the ground next to the fallen gun.

I tossed the hatchet away and picked up my Colt. I emptied the chamber and six shells tinkled as they hit the rocks. Retrieving a clean, spent casing, I slid it into the chamber before fishing five live rounds from my belt, and chambering them as well. "It's too dangerous to chamber all six rounds. The hammer's too touchy. If a man's not careful, he could lose a toe."

4
String Theories

Laboratory 311, home of the Waller-Lobue Particle Accelerator.

It was the perfect day for a high school field trip. The sun was shining, birds were singing, and the staff was... well, dead. All of them. Dead.

"Welcome to Laboratory 311", the tour guide had said, but when she went to check on the screams coming from the particle accelerator viewing chamber, she never came back.

To the best of our teacher's understanding, some sort of accident caused the emergency protocols to kick in. That meant a complete lock-down and containment of any breach. Now I'm trapped in the complex with the other students and our teacher, Mr. Panacharian, waiting for a rescue team.

"Kids, please stay together," Mr. Pan said gruffly. Pan was a big man. He wasn't fat, but he wasn't muscle-bound either. He was powerful looking, with huge hands and an overly expressive unibrow that looked like two caterpillars practicing the Kama Sutra on his forehead. Picture a Greco-Roman wrestler, but shorter. Probably just a higher concentration of Neanderthal DNA. I mean, give the man a cigar and mutton chops, and he would have been the perfect guy to play a comic book accurate Wolverine.

"Mr. Pan, I have to go to the restroom," Becky Anderson whined. *"Really bad."*

Pan's shoulders drooped, and he sighed like a man whose job it was to tell the world that humanity was on the brink of extinction. "Becky, we're supposed to remain in this room until someone comes to let us out. I don't think anyone will hold an accident against you. To be honest, I have to go too."

Brad Wilson, team quarterback, snickered. "Don't be too sure of that. I'm sure there'll be plenty of judging."

Pan swiveled his head on the tree stump serving as his neck and glared at Brad. "Don't be a dick, Brad," he said, clearly unafraid of potential repercussions. "You've been doing the pee-pee dance for the last twenty minutes."

The rest of the class, including Becky, laughed as Brad's face flushed a deep, warm crimson.

It took a moment to register amidst the laughter, but a hush rolled through the room as we all recognized the sound of what could best be described as a guttural, primal roar. The roar echoed through the room like a train passing through an underground terminal, and Becky began to cry. I put my arm around her, hoping to provide a little comfort, but I wasn't feeling all that comfortable myself.

A series of shrieks and screams rang out in the halls, followed by a high-pitched squeal that sounded like the mating call of a cyborg dolphin. Becky, voice shaking like a Yahtzee cup, whispered, "Brad just peed himself."

~

We stood in the closest thing to silence we could muster. I mean, there were whimpers, whispers, and outright crying, and of course Mr. Pan was busy hushing all of the above, but it wasn't as bad as the pandemonium going on in the hall and particle accelerator chamber.

Suddenly, the door from the adjoining viewing room flew open and a tall Japanese man wearing a lab coat and yellow safety glasses stumbled through. He quickly closed the door behind him and cursed when he remembered there wasn't a lock on our side. He turned to look at us, seeming surprised for a moment, and then wheezed, "The field trip! Thank God. Are you all accounted for?" He looked to Mr. Pan for an answer, his eyes desperate.

"Everyone's here, except Jodi, our tour guide," Mr. Pan replied. He looked just as shaken as the man standing in front of us. His name tag identified him as Fuun Shishido – Senior Controls Engineer. "Can you tell us what's happening here?"

Fuun shook his head. "Classified," he muttered.

Mr. Pan wasn't a fan of the engineer's answer. In one solid move, he hefted him against the unlocked door by the front of his lab coat. "I have more than a dozen kids here whose parents won't give a good god-damn about your classified crap! What in the *hell* is going on out there!?"

Fuun looked at us through cockeyed safety glasses. As if finally seeing us for what we were – a bunch of clueless kids who just wanted to go home – he sighed and relented. "Let go of my jacket, please."

It was a request, not a demand, and Mr. Pan obliged.

"Thank you," Fuun said, offering a slight bow. "I'm sorry. You see, *everything* is classified, even the number of sugars I take in my coffee. Chalk it up to habit." The man looked around the room. Seeing nothing but terror, he continued. He must have thought Mr. Pan was a priest, because he spilled the beans on everything *except* how many sugars he'd taken in his coffee that morning. "A strange black stone, unlike anything we'd ever seen. A power source beyond comprehension. We used it to power the accelerator. It worked well the first time. It opened the multiverse like a beautiful patchwork. We could see everything, everywhere. But the second time, the investors got greedy. They wanted to do more than just see. They wanted to explore. But it was an accident. An accident ripped a hole in the complex fabric of spacetime, and it appears the multiverse is now collapsing into a single nexus. That nexus is our lab. It's contained for the moment, but the strain of the entire multiverse pressing against the tear is just too much for even spacetime to hold. The rip is expanding. Soon it will exceed the confines of this facility, and there will be no place to hide."

"Unless someone closes it," I said matter-of-factly. I was trying to impress Becky, who'd clamped onto my arm like a human vice; a very pretty, incredibly nice smelling human vice. But it was still a valid statement, right?

Everyone in the room looked at me like I'd just professed my virginity or something.

"Seriously? Are you going to tell me you can't close it," I asked.

"He's got a point," Brad said, no longer trying to hide the drying stain on the front of his Levis.

I hadn't really expected validation from anyone, especially Brad.

Fuun sighed and pursed his lips. "I'm only a controls engineer. I'm not allowed to operate the systems necessary to-"

"Doesn't matter if you *should* do it." The new voice was Jamal Stone, a generally quiet self-described science nerd, who probably understood what was happening better than anyone on the field trip, including Mr. Pan. "The question is, *can* you?"

Fuun looked really nervous. He was obviously a rules guy. But we were teenagers. We broke rules for breakfast.

Jamal continued. "Look, I've been taking particle physics classes through MIT's online program since junior high. If you need an assistant, I've got your back. But you've got to be straight with us, alright bro?"

Fuun nodded. "Yes. It is worth a try. I think dodging any sort of liability went out the window when the rip appeared, and as far as I can tell, I'm the only employee left alive. I'll try, and I'll take whatever help I can get."

Becky was looking at Jamal with a newfound level of admiration. We all were. I'd had a crush on Becky since the fourth grade, but unless her last name was Higgs-Boson, Jamal wouldn't have even known she was alive.

I stepped forward once more. "Are there any weapons around here? Like a security station or anything? Someone has to keep everyone else safe while you guys figure this thing out."

Fuun nodded. "Yes, but I wouldn't bother with the security station. They've only got tasers and batons. There's another chamber, not far from here, with tactical exploration gear, just in case we were successful."

Mr. Pan shook his head ruefully. "Looks like you were successful."

I nodded. "Jamal, you help Mr. Susudio. Whoever wants to come with me, I'm going for the tactical gear."

Becky squeezed my arm, Jamal all but forgotten. "I'm coming with you."

Brad stepped forward bravely. "I'm with you too, nerd." His facade of bravado was as thin as our survival odds.

"Not so fast, kids." Mr. Pan put up his hands. "I'm responsible for all of you, so-"

"No disrespect, Mr. Pan," I said, "but things are only getting worse out there, and time is not on our side. You can't stop us all. If you want to protect us, come with us and gear up."

Several kids agreed out loud. While the screaming outside had ceased, the alarms continued to blare at a, well, alarming level.

Mr. Pan looked flustered, but he couldn't argue, not about that, not considering what we all knew. He finally nodded and looked at Shishido. "Ok, some of us will get the tactical gear. The rest will assist you and Jamal." He glanced around the room at my classmates. "Or stay out of the way."

A few of the students who were neither scientifically inclined, nor particularly excited about carrying a firearm, nodded sheepishly.

Mr. Pan looked satisfied. "So, Mr. Shishido, tell me. Where is this munitions depot?"

~

A few minutes later, eight of us, including Mr. Pan, Brad, Becky, and I, escaped the locked room using Mr. Shishido's keycard. He had limited access inside the facility, meaning the keycard wasn't going to open any exits leading to the outside world, but he assured us he had access to the munitions room. It turns out our humble Mr. Shishido was more important than he made himself out to be. Our unwitting savior had overseen the development of most of the systems that controlled everyday life at Waller-Lobue, including security. His card allowed him to go anywhere his expertise might be needed. Apparently, he was needed just about everywhere.

Shishido, Jamal, and the other five kids remained in the waiting area, as there were unimaginable horrors lurking on the other side of the unlocked door leading to the lab; horrors yours truly needed to take down before the science nerds could repair the rip. We wedged a chair under the doorknob, effectively preventing any accidental openings. Unfortunately, if something in the lab had even a bit of upper body strength and an inkling of determination, the chair wouldn't stop it for long.

As it turns out, Mr. Pan was a former marine, and pretty badass. We won't talk about the time he ran out of a classroom full of kids during an earthquake. Everyone's allowed a phobia. Interdimensional cosmic horror, it seemed, wasn't one of his. As part of the first marine raider battalion, clearing rooms was second nature to our warrior turned science teacher. Had we been learning from freakin' MacGyver all along?

"Stay close, kids," Pan whispered.

With the alarms still blaring, I doubt anyone but those of us closest to him could hear. He used hand signals to guide us. Even if most of us didn't know what the signals actually meant, his body language told us everything we needed to know. Two fingers up, three fingers sideways, who the hell knew, but when his hand shot up like a high-five as he was about to turn down another hall, we all recognized *stop*.

Pan looked back to see if the path behind us was clear. He raised two fingers and circled them in the air. Maybe he wanted us to turn around? Before any of us could register the signal, a mass of wet, albino-white tentacles that resembled extra-long ears of overcooked, slimy white corn, slithered around the corner, and coiled around Mr. Pan's ankle and calf. Our teacher grunted. Impressive, considering the rest of us would've shrieked like babies if the things touched us. He tried to kick at the tentacles, before realizing that was the worst possible response. Once he lifted his foot, whatever was attached to the tentacles yanked him off-balance and dragged him, screaming and flailing his arms like a cartoon character, down the hall and out of sight.

Then we all shrieked like babies.

~

The shrieking, it turned out, was also a bad idea.

A high-pitched chittering sound, followed by a rapid succession of wet, guttural yelps, echoed from somewhere in the corridor behind us. Stan Bautista, a big, quiet Samoan dude with hair like John Travolta in that really old movie, *Grease*, ran from the back of the group, towards the corridor Mr. Pan just disappeared down.

And the stampede was on.

Becky started running before I did. I only started moving because she was pulling on my arm, and one of us was bound to fall if I didn't go with her. I might have started pumping my legs like a madman when an odd clicking, like the sound of hundreds of tiny feet running, began swarming up the hall in our direction.

The problem was, everyone was running down the wrong hall. Mr. Pan had the map, but I'd memorized it. The hall our teacher disappeared down, where the class was now running, was the wrong one. We were supposed to go *straight, not left.*

I pulled on Becky and hollered, "This is the wrong way!"

She slowed and looked at me, and finally stopped. Brad and Stan, who'd inadvertently started the exodus, stopped as well. Everyone else kept running, unable to hear my shout over the alarms and screaming.

I tugged at Becky's arm, nodding back to the hall we'd come from. Without another word or gesture, the four of us ran back and turned left. As we passed through the junction of intersecting halls, I spotted Mr. Shishido's keycard on the ground. Poor Mr. Pan dropped it when the tentacles pulled him off his feet. I scooped up the card and kept running.

Then I made the mistake of looking back. About two or three dozen pregnant cat-sized creatures stopped at the juncture we'd just run back through. I tugged at Becky and shushed, pointing back down the hall. I wasn't she could even see the gesture in the dim emergency lighting. We stopped, transfixed by the mind-numbing sight. Brad and Stan stopped and looked back as well. There was a collective skipped heartbeat as we watched. Suddenly, Brad wasn't the only one with pee in his pants. Hey! It might be Stan I'm talking about, or Becky. No judging, alright?

Oh, yeah, the creatures. The creatures looked like they were very, very distant relatives to spiders. Their bodies were roughly the size of volleyballs, and their color was a sickly, translucent, milky hue, like an amphibian's eggs. We could see through to their innards. While their skin was clear, there was an awful mixture of red and pink tones swirling around in what looked like their digestive tract. Most likely human flesh. Becky dug her nails into my forearm. I was fairly sure I was bleeding by now. The bodies were bad enough, but their legs made me wish I was wearing brown pants. It's a pirate joke my dad likes to tell. Look it up. Their legs were long and spindly, but sturdy looking. They were the same milky white hue, and covered with spiky, white hairs that seemed to move independently, like a cat's whiskers. The worst thing about the legs wasn't the length, the color, or the fact they needed a waxing in the worst way. It wasn't even that they had so many we couldn't count them. It was the tiny tongues. From each joint, on each leg, *and there were a lot of both*, what looked like a tiny tongue protruded, licking eagerly at the air, tasting it. Maybe smelling it? And it might have been the diffused lighting, but I couldn't seem to see a single eye on any of the things. They appeared to be blind.

The four of us had stopped in the hall, right out in plain sight. We'd be sitting ducks if the things decided to come our way. As I said, though, the things had to have been blind, because they'd stopped at the T-juncture, seemingly confused by the two directions available to them. Their tiny tongues lapped at the air, like a cat at a puddle of milk, and their leg whiskers moved as if pushed by an unseen wind. Then the tapping started again. It was nothing in comparison to the awfulness of the alarms, but it was so consistent and rhythmic that the emergency systems couldn't overshadow it. The sound was like hundreds of tiny tap dancers sending out messages in Morse code. But creepier, like if the tap dancers were mimes.

Then someone farted.

I refuse to believe it was Becky, even though she excused herself. It must have been Stan or Brad. She was just being polite.

But when one of the two cretins cut the cheese, the collective tap dancing monstrosities' whiskers all swayed in our direction, and a thousand tiny tongues started licking at the air in our section of the hall.

Then they took a step towards us. And when I say they, I mean *all* of them.

One step became two, two became four, and before we knew it, they were practically skipping in our direction singing "Zippity Doodah". I don't know about them, but I wanted to go away from the fart, not towards it.

Several more steps and the multi-legged nightmares were practically on top of us. The way we huddled together, if they brushed past one of us, they'd find us all.

I lifted my foot to step on the closest one, though I was certain all that would do was make it mad. Seeing as we were already doomed.

Then we heard the roar, the screams, and the stampede of footsteps coming from Mr. Pan Memorial Hallway. Our classmates found something else, or something else found them. The spiderlings decided the screaming and running was far more interesting than a fart. Without so much as a 'see y'all later', they were off to dinner.

A moment later, the screaming increased. A few seconds after that, everything became quiet again.

~

"Move," I whisper-shouted.

We continued our panicked race towards the safety of the munitions room. A shriek from behind us froze us in our tracks. It was human.

We turned to see Aleah Lopez stumbling towards us, her eyes wide with terror. She screamed again when she saw us and reached out for help.

We all bolted towards her, but stopped short when we saw the opaque, whisker covered leg stalks creeping over her shoulders and around her upper torso. The whiskers seemed to do nothing to the fabric of her hoodie, but as soon as they touched the exposed flesh of her neck and face, they burrowed in like sentient porcupine quills. They pulled the legs and those awful flicking tongues up against her neck and face, but that was just the terrifying beginning. As the legs made contact, Aleah's flesh dissolved like a hot knife passing through a hard stick of butter, or maybe a lightsaber through metal. There was definitely some bubbling. Man, I don't mean to sound callous. Seriously, in that awful moment, I think the four of us screamed at least as much as Aleah. She was our friend. We grew up together. I still remember the first day of kindergarten. Aleah sat next to me. We got in trouble for talking. The photographer had to take a second picture because of us.

We could only assume Mr. Pan, Tegan Short, and Karsten Jablonka were dead. In Aleah's case, though, we were sure of it. We had to watch her die. Her voice suddenly turned into a gurgling spurt, and it was over.

Bile filled my mouth at a ratio equivalent to the tears filling my eyes.

Becky was shaking uncontrollably. "Oh my God! Oh my God!"

I hugged her tightly. "We're going to be alright. Right, guys?" I looked to Stan and Brad for reassurance.

They were holding each other the way Becky was holding me. Brad let go of Stan. "Not a word, nerd! Do you hear me?"

Stan looked like he still needed a hug.

"Yeah," I stammered. It wasn't time for jokes. "Not a word, man. I promise."

We all backed away from Aleah's corpse and the thing that was greedily consuming her. More pink and red swirls appeared in its digestive tract, these shades fresh, and darker than the previous ones.

For a moment the thing stopped feeding, its whiskers pointed towards us like tiny magnets, feeling the air currents, perhaps. The horrible tongues, now dripping with bits of our friend's flesh and bone, lapped tentatively at the air that existed between us. I hoped nobody else had to fart. Then, as if satisfied, it continued dining on Aleah. Of course, that wasn't the end of it. How could it have been? As it continued dissolving and absorbing, it began to tap a foot on the concrete floor beneath Aleah's body. The pattern was rhythmic, almost hypnotic.

Suddenly, more tapping echoed from the distant, darkened hallway beyond it. It was as if the others were... answering?

Then it dawned on me. The reason it sounded like Morse code. The tapping wasn't just echolocation. It was a form of communication!

"Run," I barked. "Now!"

The four of us ran like our lives depended on it. Believe

me, they did! The tapping had started as a response, but as soon

as we began running, it increased in volume. The spiderlings were

in pursuit once again.

~

We tore down the hall at breakneck speed. Becky let go of

my arm and pulled ahead of all of us. Brad, everybody's favorite

quarterback, was close behind Becky, then me, and finally poor

Stan, who was not exactly a track and field star.

We rounded another corner, and I called out to Becky and

Brad, who had both run past the door to the munitions room. The

alarm was still blaring, and Becky didn't hear me. Brad grabbed

the back of her sweater, almost pulling it off. Becky screamed and

batted at Brad's hand.

"It's okay," Brad shouted. "It's just me!"

Becky looked around, panicked beyond any real rationality or reason, but when she saw me open the door and let Stan run through, she swatted Brad's hand away and ran back to the safety of the munitions room.

Becky practically dove through the doorway. Brad, not to be outdone by a girl, slid through the opening like a baseball player stealing first. Finally, I ducked inside and slammed the door behind me.

As I locked the door, I felt something touch my shoe. I looked down and leapt back, revolted by the sight and the smell. It was about eight inches of a spiderling's leg. I'd cut it off cleanly when I slammed the door. A clear substance the consistency of melted Vaseline oozed from the open end of the severed leg.

Brad inched forward, reaching out to touch it.

I grabbed his wrist. "Dude, look," I said, my breath hitching after our mad dash for freedom.

As Brad extended his fingers, the whiskers stiffened, like they were straining to reach him. The worst possible high five ever.

"It's still trying to eat," Stan commented behind Brad.

Becky tried to turn on some lights, but the emergency lighting was apparently all we were going to get. Thankfully, there were no alarm speakers wired into the munitions room, though we could hear them through the door just as clearly as we could hear the incessant, nerve-grinding tapping.

Brad pulled his hand away, his face betraying the all too fresh memory of Aleah's horrible death. I suddenly felt awful for her parents.

"It's still alive," Brad wondered out loud.

"Probably more like a worm's physiology," Becky commented, still sounding shaken, but calmer than before. She was on a biology track. She'd probably be a doctor one day if we survived long enough to turn in college applications. "Their digestive system seems to run throughout its entire body, so it's more like a worm or a plant, than anything else."

Brad shuddered. "Gross."

Becky shrugged. "You've heard of the book, *Everyone Poops*, right? Well, everyone eats, too."

"Enough about the damned spider leg," I said. We had more pressing matters than theoretical alien biology at stake.

"It's not really a spider-" Becky started.

"Fine," I snapped, suddenly wishing I hadn't used that tone with her. "Sorry. I'm just worried about the others, and the fate of the world. You know? We need to sort out these weapons and get back to them, so they can close the rip."

Becky looked surprised. So did Brad and Stan. I was generally pretty chill.

"It's okay," Becky said finally. "We're all on edge." She walked over to the wall of weapons and gestured at them. "Any idea what any of this is?"

Stan raised a hand, forgetting he wasn't in class. "Yeah, my uncle's a survival freak. I spent a few summers with him and my cousins in Montana. I never actually thought those summers might save my life one day."

"Or save the world," Brad muttered.

"Well then, Stan, my friend," I said, intentionally lightening up my tone. "The floor's yours. What have we got here?"

~

Stan wasn't kidding about his time in Montana. Aside from a few items that were more science-related than search and destroy, Stan could identify everything, right down to the ammo. The room was like a Toys R' Us for the Unabomber. Lining the walls were guns, ammo, grenades, flamethrowers, RPGs, landmines, various types of goggles and scopes, even bladed weapons, like machetes, survival shovels, and axes. Then there was the survival gear itself. Fatigues, enviro-suits, oxygen tanks, MREs and water packs, medical kits, the list went on and on.

"Get into an enviro-suit and load up a duffle bag with everything you can carry while still using a gun," I said, feeling a lot like Winston Churchill, but less inspiring.

Becky stood looking at the enviro-suits. She was clearly uncomfortable with the idea of putting one on. She saw me looking at her and blushed. "I'm sorry," she said quietly. "I'm super claustrophobic. I can't even play hide and seek without a panic attack."

I smiled and lied. "Me too. But we don't want those spi-uh, wormie-plantie thingies that look like effed up spiders to touch our skin, right?"

She nodded. "Yeah, you're right."

"Want us to turn around," I asked, nodding at Brad and Stan, who were already picking out enviro-suits.

Becky wrinkled her nose. "Why? Because you might see my bra?"

It was my turn to blush.

"We don't have time for vanity, Packard," she said, pulling off her sweater and top.

Aaaaaand I saw her bra.

5
String Theories: Sector 2
The Particle Accelerator

Stan laid on his stomach at the back of the room, an M2 Browning — a .50 caliber badass mo-fo were Stan's exact words — positioned on a low, wide-based tripod in front of him, aimed directly at the door. Brad and Becky were hunkered behind a metal table we'd upended and set up as a potential line of defense against the spiderlings and whatever else might have joined the unholy, alien congregation in the hall. They were both armed and ready to fire at the potential wave of monsters, just like Stan taught us. And me? Well, like a dumbass, I volunteered to open the door. I mean, I had grenades to throw into the hall, and I was ready to dive behind the table with Brad and Becky as Stan unloaded his .50 cal on the bastards. But hey, somebody had to open the door.

Why not me?

To my dismay, the evil, tap-dancing mimes were still in the hall, and the alarms were still blaring like angel's trumpets announcing the end of the world.

"On three," Stan finally whispered, disengaging the safety and gripping the twin handles with both hands.

Brad and Becky, heads and guns sticking out from behind the table, were ready to join in the action if necessary. They looked like something straight out of an old World War II movie. It was like trench warfare, but in a big, concrete conference room. A conference room with guns on the wall... like a conference for gangsters... aw hell, you know what I mean.

"One."

No turning back now.

"Two."

My feet felt like lead. I wasn't sure I'd be able to move once I'd pulled the door open. I was about to find ou-

"Three!"

I turned the knob and pulled. The minute or so that followed was probably the worst and longest of my life.

More than a dozen spiderlings practically fell through the doorway. Before I could enjoy tossing a grenade into the opaque mass of legs, tongues, and bodies, Stan began firing his beast of a gun. Spent casings pinged to the floor by the dozen, and I suddenly understood what it would be like to work in the quality control department testing Zeus's lightning bolts. To say the sound was deafening would be a gross understatement. My eardrums felt like speaker cones at a metal concert. To add insult to injury, or just to pile on more injury, the shrapnel and body parts produced by the constant spray of bullets was like cleaning up a driving range while the golfers were still practicing their swings. Legs, guts, Vaseline-blood, and golf ball sized chunks of concrete and wood pelted my legs repeatedly.

I dove behind the table and found Becky and Brad screaming. At least I think they were screaming. Their mouths were open like they were screaming, but all any of us could hear was Stan's 90 pound monster-shredder. The firing slowed for a moment while Stan fed another belt of ammo into the gun. I think I heard Stan laughing in that brief moment. Good for him, man. Good for him.

A minute or so later, the spiderlings, the door, and the walls surrounding it were no more.

The firing stopped, but my ears would be ringing for days to come. Stan suddenly put a hand on my shoulder. I looked up and met his eyes. He gestured towards the duffle bags behind us. I tapped on Brad and Becky's shoulders, nodding towards the bags.

It was time to go.

~

After loading up, the four of us moved stealthily up the corridor towards the particle accelerator and the rest of our friends. One thought dominated all others as we headed towards an uncertain future, and all-too certain doom. *Pink! Her bra was pink!*

Our enviro-suits were combat ready, and the helmets outfitted with small, but powerful LED spotlights around the face shields. The added light made the run back to the lab a lot easier to navigate, though I really didn't want to see the spiderlings better. The gloves were thin but surprisingly durable, and allowed us to feel the triggers of our guns without having to apply any added pressure.

We each carried an M27 — a U.S. Marine's standard issue machine gun — and a duffle bag. Our chosen weapons each sported a bayonet, a suppressor, and a laser sight. Inside our duffle bags, we carried several 30-round magazines, MREs and water, a combat shovel — yeah, it's really a thing — and several grenades. Stan gave each of us a different flavor of grenade, so we wouldn't get them confused and throw the wrong type in the heat of battle. Mine were standard fragmentation grenades. Brad got flash-bangers; all bright, but very little heat. Becky opted for the less lethal smoke variety. Stan carried the HEs – high intensity – which he explained would be a bit like bathing in a solar flare. He also picked up an RPG and three projectiles. RPG is short for rocket propelled grenade, which is basic anti-tank gear in the outside world. I guess, technically, Stan chose two flavors of grenades.

It was crazy to think that, at one time or another, Stan had actually played with everything we collectively carried. Just when you think you know someone.

~

Surprisingly, we didn't run into any other interdimensional monstrosities on our return trip to Mr. Shishido and our six friends in the waiting room. I guessed there'd been a breach along the north or west wall of the lab, someplace next to the Mr.

Panacharian Memorial Hallway. There was probably another somewhere on the east side, which allowed the spiderlings to flank us from behind.

Halfway to the waiting room, we realized we could hear the glorious sound of our own running feet. It was odd to hear, since the constant droning of the alarms had become an accepted condition, like humidity you could hear instead of feel. It was awful, but you got used to it. Just as suddenly as they blared to life, the alarms shut down.

There were always two sides to every coin. The flip side of our alarm vs. silence coin was that the multi-legged beasties and other things that went bump in the night could hear us now. No more alarm bells to confuse them.

We finally reached the waiting room and were shocked to find it empty. The chair we'd placed against the doorknob had been flung across the little room and lay bent in a corner. The door leading to the lab hung by a single hinge. Dim light filtered eerily through the opening in a smoky gray haze, and there was a smeared, bloody handprint on the once pristine, white door.

"Same plan as before," Stan whispered, though he didn't have to. We had two-way com units built into our helmets. No one else could hear us unless we shouted. "Pack gets the door. I'll be the first through, since I'm the best shot. Pack, you fall back and cover Becky and Brad as they follow me through. Becky, go left as you enter. Brad, you go right. Remember, barrels angled down and fingers off the triggers unless you're firing. It'll be easy to mistake survivors, and each other, for monsters once we're in there. Friendly fire is a no-no. Pack, you bring up the rear. I'll provide cover fire for all of you as you enter, and then take to high ground as soon as I'm able."

We all nodded before I added, "Be careful to not damage systems necessary to close the rip. Assuming anyone's still alive in there who knows how."

"Good call, Pack," Stan agreed. "Now, let's go kick some interdimensional ass."

~

The statement, 'nothing ever goes as planned', was coined for a reason. I feel like someone had me in mind when the words were first uttered. There's even a classic rock song by the band Styx explaining the concept. They could have dedicated it to me.

For the record, I followed the plan to the letter. I got in close to the door, looked for movement beyond the narrow opening, and then kicked it in.

I really didn't ever want to see the spiderlings up close, but we don't always get what we want now, do we? The moment I kicked in the door, three things happened simultaneously. First, a wet mass of tentacles wrapped around my ankles, pulling my feet together and dropping me to the floor. As I hit the concrete, several spiderlings swarmed over me, their tiny, transparent tongues lapping at my bio-suit, looking for an opening. Then the door ripped free of its remaining hinge, almost knocking me out as it fell on me.

Stan rushed through, careful not to step on the door, but before he could lift the heavy slab of metal off me, Becky and Brad followed. Not surprisingly, they both managed to trample me like a herd of elephants running over a sloth at nap time. Normally, I'd be less than pleased with their carelessness but, under the circumstances, I was appreciative. Somehow, they'd managed to squash the entire swarm of spiderlings, covering me with their corrosive Vaseline blood and all the pink and red chunks that made up their lunch. I laid there covered with gore and unable to move. Suddenly, a hulking figure erupted boldly from the smoke and shadows. It was Mr. Pan! He held a firefighter's axe mid-handle, looking like a warrior dwarf from a Tolkien book, only beardless and a tad-bit taller. Covered in blood, grime, and soot, he looked like he'd just been dragged straight through hell by his hair.

He reached down with his free hand and tossed the door aside like it was cardboard. Then he held out the blade of his axe, nodding towards it. I grasped it tightly and he pulled me to my feet. He was careful to keep the spiderling's blood and guts off his skin.

"We thought you were dead!" I hollered through the mask.

"I should be," he hollered back. "But I discovered the tentacles don't like it when their prey bites back. They taste like shit. *Zero stars*. Would not recommend, kiddo."

I would have laughed if I wasn't so scared. I looked down at the mention of the tentacles, panicking. As it turned out, spiderlings and their secretions were just as dangerous to the tentacles, as they were to us. The tentacles slowly melted off my legs like the chocolate bar I left on my dad's dashboard last summer.

Stan climbed the scaffolding that surrounded the accelerator chamber, looking for a high-ground position. Becky and Brad stopped when they saw our teacher. We all focused our attention on him. Becky finally spoke, probably louder than she wanted to. "Aleah's dead, Mr. Pan. We saw it happen. It was horrible."

Pan's expression softened when he heard the words. "Dammit," he finally muttered. "Karsten? Tegan?"

"They ran off with her," Brad replied. "We haven't seen them since."

Pan shook his head and sighed. He pointed back through the smoke and a mass of sparking wires. "I looped around the halls and found my way here through a break in the wall behind the accelerator. I haven't seen anyone else until you showed up."

Becky held out her gun to Mr. Pan. "Wanna trade?"

He lit up at the sight of the M27, and eagerly handed Becky the axe in return. "Be careful," he said. "The safety's off."

Looking confused, Becky studied the axe. Then she looked at him, rolling her eyes, the faintest hint of a smile curling the edges of her lips. "Funny, Mr. Pan."

His eyes twinkled. He loved being a teacher, probably even more than he'd loved being a Marine, but given the choice between the M27 and a dry-erase marker, there was obviously no contest.

"I found them," Stan called from the scaffolding. Everyone except Mr. Pan turned. He didn't have the benefit of a two-way radio in his helmet, or a helmet.

He motioned towards an enclosed glass chamber about twenty feet into the room. From what I could see through the haze, it appeared to be a control room. There were lots of flashing lights and stuff, but hey, what did I know?

"Mr. Pan," I shouted. When he looked at me, I pointed at the glass enclosure. "Stan says he found the others in there!"

"Tell Pan and the others I'll cover them. You cover me while I climb back down," Stan's voice crackled in my helmet.

"Roger that," I replied. *I always wanted to say that.*

Mr. Pan motioned for Brad and Becky to go ahead of him, then turned to me. "Go with them," he said. "You're my responsibility. I'm not losing another one of you."

I shook my head, dropping Mr. Shishido's keycard in his hand. "Get them to safety, Mr. Pan. Stan has us covered. I'll cover him as he joins us. We'll be right behind you."

Mr. Pan's lips drew into a thin line. He was ready to argue but realized Becky and Brad were already ahead of him. He pointed at me, his expression serious to a fault. "Get Stan down. I'll cover both of you and bring you home. Got it?"

"Yessir!" I saluted him. It felt weird, not actually being military, but then Mr. Pan saluted back.

Without another word, he lumbered off towards the glass enclosure.

"I've got you covered, Stan," I whispered over the com-link. "You're a go, big guy."

Stan didn't answer. He just started climbing like his life depended on it. It took a few moments. By the time he reached the floor, Pan, Becky, and Brad were in the control room.

As soon as Becky and Brad were inside, Pan came back out and waved for us to join him.

Stan was almost to the enclosure when something roared from the opposite side of the room. The roar shook the walls around us like a runaway freight train tearing through a tunnel.

We all turned to face the source of the noise. It was a lump of clear tissue the size of an elephant. Tentacles, the ones plaguing us since back in the hallway, covered the thing's body.

The tentacles stretched and ran their suckers over every exposed surface as the beast moved forward. It didn't seem to need the tentacles to move. While they felt and grabbed things around it, something like a giant snail's foot simultaneously pulled and pushed it across the floor. It was like a giant octoslug. No, too many tentacles. A centeslug maybe?

Stan began firing at the thing, but bullets didn't seem to faze it. It was like shooting spitballs at a lump of sour cream. The bullets simply struck, then fell away, like raindrops off a window... a slimy, scary window.

Suddenly, the thing began to draw in air, expanding like a slowly inflating balloon. Then, without any warning, centeslug rapidly expelled the air through unseen orifices all over its body. The sound was like an unholy union between a fart and a

T. rex's roar. The noise was terrifying enough, but the orifices also shot out some horrifying clear jelly that, like the spiderling's secretions, seemed to have corrosive properties. Unlike the spiderlings though, the corrosion was not exclusive to organic tissue. Desks, walls, wires, *entire sections of floor*, melted away.

I watched in awe and terror as the thing bulldozed through the lab, tentacles waving wildly in all directions, roaring and spewing as it went, like Moby Dick wrestling a giant squid.

Then the unthinkable happened. Stan hollered, *"Get down!"*

The command crackled in my headset like a poorly tuned radio station. I turned to see him firing off one of the RPG projectiles. I threw my hands in the air, but it was too late.

The rocket struck the centeslug center mass, and the concussive force of the explosion was nothing short of devastating. The bullets had been ineffective at worst, an irritation at best, but the RPG was not a gun. The monster blew apart like a cherry bomb planted in jello salad. The creature's disintegrating body hit Mr. Pan first. He vaporized before our eyes, without enough time to even scream. I turned to see Stan's enviro-suit melting around him, and then he was melting too. Stan, unfortunately, did have time to scream. I couldn't hear him for long. The next moment brought screams to my own lips. Little did I know, corrosive awfulness covered my helmet. It took mere seconds to eat right through. Pain like I'd never imagined possible ripped through my body like the otherworldly roars of the centeslug. My face disappeared like a marshmallow left in the fire too long, and before I could die, I passed out from the pain.

Game over.

6

GIFTED

I caught my breath, an irrational wave of fear washing over me, like when you wake up from a nightmare you're on the cusp of forgetting.

All I could recall was my face burning before the dream faded like a sigh in a hurricane.

It took a moment to gather my bearings, but before long the Earth came back into focus, and I remembered where I was. Safely soaring high above the planet I'd sworn to protect with my life. To date, I hadn't found anything that could even remotely harm me, except maybe old age. I do age, slowly, but eventually entropy even catches up with superheroes. Entropy is the real grim reaper.

The world's beautiful from up here — just a big blue marble, with white swirls over odd-shaped patches of gray, brown, and green. I had a cat-eye marble that looked like it when I was a kid. Somewhere down there, it still existed. Maybe in a landfill, in the backyard of my old house, or even in the possession of some new lucky child, but it still existed. That's the nature of matter and the law of conservation of mass. Entropy be damned. When I eventually cease being me, my molecules will become something else. Hopefully, something amazing.

But for now, and I expect for a very long time, I am the Golden Sentinel, sworn defender of Earth and her almost eight billion inhabitants.

I floated quietly, miles above the surface of the breathtaking blue planet, watching, listening. My pristine white cape floated loosely around me, as there was no atmosphere to disturb it, nor gravity to tug at its hem.

Let me tell you, when it rains, it most definitely pours. In my case, it usually hails, sleets, snows, and throws in some frogs and locusts for good measure. The world went from relatively quiet – you know, stuff the global police forces and militaries can safely deal with – to absolute hell in a handbasket in a matter of seconds. Only this handbasket is almost a hundred and ninety-seven million square miles. That's a huge handbasket for Hell to eff-up.

You can plan and prepare, but much like the Spanish Inquisition, you can never actually expect the unexpected. That's why it's called the unexpected. Trust me, my life revolves around it.

As I was saying, the world went from quietly sleeping baby to colicky quintuplets in the blink of an eye.

It all started with a volcano erupting on the island of Nea Kameni, a tiny island in the cluster that makes up Santorini, Greece. Hundreds of tourists would be in the path of any resulting lava flow, and traditional evacuation processes would be too late, so it was a priority-one emergency.

Before I could fly in and save the day, though, the city of San Francisco, all the way over on the West Coast of the United States, began to shake like one of those tacky hula dancer figurines people put on the dashboard of their car. San Francisco's car clearly had bad shocks and was driving through potholes.

To make matters worse, a massive sinkhole nearly a mile in diameter suddenly formed in the Sea of Japan. Midway between Japan and South Korea, the liquid black hole guzzled seawater like a beer drinker at a football game. Its gaping maw pulled in a luxury liner, the ship's superstructure shuddering and groaning as it careened sideways.

As I formulated a plan of attack, yet another hero-sized event let down its unruly hair. A small, undetectable fragment of meteorite struck the JEM – Japanese Experimental Module – of the International Space Station. The damage was so minor, the naked eye could barely see it. However, in a very short time, that segment of the ISS's artificial atmosphere would fail, and all the current residents of the JEM would suffer an unpleasant demise.

I could see all this happening from where I floated, but even with my awesome speed and strength, I'd never figured out how to be in more than one place at a time.

The space station was closest, but there were people on the western coast of Nea Kameni bathing in the tantalizing warmth of the natural hot springs.

Moving at speeds rivaling light itself, I hurried off to save the day.

~

I arrived on the coast of Nea Kameni a fraction of a second later, and not a moment too soon. The people in the hot springs were already shouting that the water suddenly felt uncomfortably hot. In mere seconds it would become toxic and start to boil.

As cool as my superpowers are, nature imposes some practical limits on how I can use them. I can only move as fast as whatever I'm carrying can handle. Too fast, and the friction would tear them apart, like a stack of papers flying off the roof of a speeding car, so no speed of light travel while carrying a person. I know what you're thinking. Yes, I did learn that lesson the hard way. Cut me some slack though. It's not like there's a school for superheroes or anything!

Around five to six hundred miles per hour is my max speed when carrying a human being unless they're inside a structure that can withstand greater speeds. Then it's on. We can go all sorts of fast. Like tens of thousands of miles per hour, depending on the structural integrity of the thing they're enclosed in.

I don't have some magical aura that extends out and protects anything I'm touching, like in the comics. That's just silly. The laws of physics still apply, friends, just not to me. Why? Well, it's a long story, but the Cliffs Notes version says

I was gifted powers of a divine origin. Even *I* don't totally understand my powers, but I know they don't seem to have any upward limits. Strength, speed, flight, even healing. I'm a mixed bag of vanilla powers. The healing comes in handy if I'm too late to prevent injuries, but resurrection is impossible, even for me. Dead is dead. Doornails will remain doornails. As much as I desperately want to, even I can't save everyone, everywhere, all the time.

There were about forty people in and around the coastal hot spring. I zipped past the captains of the tour boats, and told them in Greek – yep, I speak every known language, including a few forgotten ones for good measure – to turn west and move like hell!

As the captains shouted out their orders, I pulled people from the water, two by two, and deposited them carefully on the boats. There were a few bathing suits lost during the rescue. *You think 500 miles per hour makes a face look funny!* In a matter of seconds, I scooped up every person in immediate danger. With a half salute, half-wave I'm pretty sure no one actually saw, I rocketed towards the distressed luxury liner in the Tsushima Strait.

~

The ship was already buckling. She would need serious structural repairs once she was back in port.

An incredible assortment of seabirds circled the sinkhole. Morbid curiosity is clearly not a trait exclusive to humans and felines. It sounded as if the people on the ship were engaged in a screaming match with the seabirds.

Speaking of screaming, a few lifeboats had dropped into the churning waters of the strait. People foolish enough to hop in before their release were being sucked rapidly towards the ravenous expanse. I flew into the frigid waters and emerged with one of the lifeboats held over my head. I deposited the small craft on a deserted upper deck, and returned to the waters twice more, each time returning with another lifeboat full of terrified men, women, and children. Once the lifeboats were up and out of the way, I shouted for everyone to get below deck. I started to turn the ship's nose away from the terrifying phenomenon. I had to turn the behemoth slowly, as she wasn't built to withstand the strain of a sudden six hundred mile per hour pivot. If I tried that, the ship would snap in two, like the Titanic, and I'd have a brand-new disaster on my hands.

I felt the clock ticking as I turned the beast south. Once I was sure everyone was below deck, I found a structurally solid spot at the rear of the ship and began to push. The effort was more than a playground shove, but nowhere near what I could without the friction of the salt water in my way. Water is far denser than most people realize and moving a skyscraper sized vessel at any significant speed is no small feat. I was strong enough to hurl the ship into space with ease if I wanted to, but those pesky laws of physics still apply. Sending her flying like a jet engine would destroy her and kill everyone on board, so I had to go slower than dial-up internet to get the ship to safety.

You might wonder why I didn't pick the ship up and fly her out of harm's way, like I did with the lifeboats. Ever try to hold a wet paper plate full of food up with the tip of your finger? Too much area and too little support. The odds of pulling it off safely were too low. I'd risk either punching through the hull or breaking the ship in half.

I pushed as fast as I could without risking the lives of the passengers, well under a hundred miles per hour. Under normal circumstances, a ship like that never exceeded thirty! It took the better part of a minute to complete my rescue of the ship and her passengers. Finally, amidst the din of grateful cheers and relieved tears, I streaked skyward, directly towards the ISS.

~

I flew in with the grace and control of a hummingbird and hovered outside the JEM. I briefly studied the damage before flying to the edge of a series of stabilizer panels. Taking hold of the edge of a thin metal panel, I bent it back and forth, like folding a piece of paper before tearing it along a scored line. Then I tore the metal. The repeated bending created a weakened line in the metal that allowed me to achieve the tear with no additional visible damage. When the world was no longer on the brink of disaster, I could go back and repair or perhaps replace the panel.

Rocketing back to the puncture in the JEM unit, I began rubbing the metal between my hands furiously, superheating the business card-sized piece to nearly three thousand degrees. I placed it against the puncture, pressing firmly enough to effectively weld the patch in place.

Satisfied the ISS was out of danger, I sped back to Earth.

~

Now, you might be thinking the citizens of San Francisco and Santorini would be toast by now, especially the tourists still on Nea Kameni. See what I did there? Volcano? Toast? Okay, that was probably in poor taste. But seriously, I'm fast. Reeeeeaaaaaly fast. I'm 'saved the entire world in the time it took you to read the last couple of pages' kinda fast, so bear with me. That was a long day.

As I raced towards the California coast, and ultimately that oh-so famous City by the Bay, I could see the region erupting into utter chaos. It wasn't massive, around a 6.2 on the Richter scale, but the quake was centered closer to the city than any since the big one of 1906. There was going to be a lot of damage. I arrived over the South Bay just as all hell broke loose.

The Golden Gate Bridge was bucking like a bull in a rodeo. Cars crashed into each other as they were pushed precariously towards the edge. A two hundred and twenty foot drop would crush a car like a bug on a windshield and kill everyone inside. Like I said before, water's harder than people realize. The seismic force tugged the support cables in directions they weren't ever meant to be tugged. If even one of them broke free, it would cut through the cars like a steel bullwhip through a piñata.

I flew the length of the bridge shouting for everyone to put up their windows and convertible tops. Then I went to work.

I needed a safe place to deposit the vehicles as I removed them from the bridge. The grassy area at the center of Fort Baker, only about a mile north, would be perfect. A similar area at the center of Fort Winfield Scott existed roughly a mile to the south.

Going slow enough to avoid injury, I could pick up a vehicle, fly it to a fort, and set it down, about once a second. Return trips, at that close distance, were virtually instantaneous when viewed by the naked eye.

A mortal couldn't follow the amount of disastrous activity going on in the city at the moment. Luckily, my powers let me

take in everything around me and process it instantly. Every brick
that tumbled, every crack that formed in every road, every broken
pane of glass, every scream and shout for help, I heard it all. In
between my deliveries of cars from the bridge to the grassy knolls,
I crisscrossed the city like a sentient beam of golden light, catching
people as they fell, shielding them from falling debris, and putting
out fires as they erupted. I placed my rescuees in the safest
possible places and zipped off to the bridge to collect more cars and
trucks.

About twenty-five seconds after the devastating shaking
began, it ceased. But the city still needed a whole lot of saving. For
every person I plucked from the crosshairs of danger, there were
hundreds, maybe thousands more, who were still in some sort of
peril. It was going to be a very busy day.

I shot around the city for another few seconds, removing
large sections of debris from atop trapped cars and clearing the way
for emergency response teams to assist. You see, I'm not the only

hero in town. There are firefighters, EMTs, police officers, doctors, nurses, and so many others, paid and unpaid, who are always instrumental in saving lives and property when disaster strikes. I get the parades and photo-ops, but honestly, those unsung heroes out there, who never share the stage or spotlight with yours truly, they're the ones who deserve the recognition. They're just as vulnerable as the people they save, yet they put their lives on the line just the same.

They're the real heroes.

~

Before anyone could thank me, assuming they'd even seen who'd saved them, I streaked back towards Santorini. I still had a volcano to deal with.

I arrived back at the island to find the magma advancing over Nea Kameni like a wave of giant fire ants, if the ants were made of actual fire. Though the tourists who chose to visit the island that fateful day were all heading for coastal waters, the wall of molten death would overtake most of them long before they could get to any real semblance of safety.

I studied the situation for a moment and decided my original plan was still the best. Diving under the crystal waters on the northernmost side of the island, I continued down until I reached the seabed, more than thirteen hundred feet below. Once there, I dug furiously into the centuries old lava rock that made up the base of the island, punching through Earth's crust to the mantle below. I dug in and upwards at a forty-degree angle, turning lava rock, and pockets of iron, nickel, and diamond into dust with my bare hands. I punched, grabbed, crushed, and brushed aside chunks of the mantle as I bored upwards, eventually reaching the magma vent that fed the volcano. The torrent of molten lava that suddenly flooded my makeshift tunnel would have destroyed most anything in its path, but to me, it barely registered as warm. The magma immediately began to flow down the tunnel, and as it did,

I followed it back towards the sea below. As I returned to the opening of the tube, I widened the tunnel's diameter, allowing more lava to flow, and ensuring it wouldn't cool too soon and impede upon the lava's new direction.

I returned to the surface and watched for a moment as the magma flowing into the sea began to form what would one day be a new island. It was rare, but occasionally even I could be impressed.

I spent the next few minutes healing tourists who'd been too close to the advancing lava and suffered first and second degree burns by sheer proximity. That's one thing I have to slow down to 'mortal time' for. The time it takes to lay my hands on someone and heal them isn't as trivial as most tasks. Besides, even if only for a moment, it's nice to look into the eyes of someone I save. It wholly reminds me why I do what I do. Every time.

A young girl from Ireland and her father were the last to receive my gift. The man was in his early thirties, and thankfully in excellent health. He and his daughter, who was about five, had been exploring the rim of the volcano when it erupted. They'd been at a safe distance under normal circumstances, but the coast was just too far for him to carry his daughter ahead of a rampaging wall of liquid heat. I've been too late before, too late to heal. Thankfully, this family was going home unscathed.

The man, Errol, had been running from the advancing wave, carrying his daughter in his arms, clutching her tightly to his chest. The heat left his back blistered and raw, bleeding in some places from the scorch marks, like Blowtorch Man had been chasing him. Yeah, he was a thing for a minute. But archenemies are a story for another time.

As painful as I knew his wounds were, Errol insisted I heal his daughter, Marjorie, first. Since her arms had been wrapped around his neck, her tiny hands and wrists were also heat blasted and raw. I held Marjorie's hands in mine and felt the power flow. Healing is as close to truly experiencing the divine nature of my powers as I ever get. It's transformative for the recipient of my gift, but almost as much for me. See, I haven't felt real pain in a very long time. When I heal someone, I can feel their pain. It's a brief flare, quick, like a paper cut, but for a moment I feel it all. I can lift buildings all day but healing actually drains me a bit. Marjorie's hands healed quickly and beautifully. She wouldn't even have a scar to remind her of her terrifying visit to Santorini.

As I placed my hands on Errol's back, I could still feel the tingle of Marjorie's burns in my fingertips. Then, for just a moment, my back flared like someone poured boiling oil over it.

In seconds, Errol's back was as good as new. I even fixed a bulging disk at L5-S1 he probably hadn't been to the doctor for yet, just for good measure.

The father and daughter looked at me with pure gratitude and awe. Marjorie touched my face, tracing my cheek with a tiny, perfect fingertip, and Errol placed a hand on my shoulder. There were tears in the man's pale blue eyes. "I can never repay what you've done for us," he said. "Bless you, friend."

He took Marjorie's hands in his own, and hefted her up, back into his arms. As they strolled towards the rescue boats in the western harbor, Marjorie waved goodbye.

And then the moment was over.

Many more moments lay ahead, though. San Francisco was still in dire need of assistance, and there were countless more people there to heal.

~

I was in the Bay Area for almost an hour; healing, digging, and rescuing. Between Santorini and San Francisco, it's amazing there were no fatalities. I take my job as sworn defender of Earth seriously, folks. Any day I can pull off rescues like that, and whisk a few fatally injured people away from the Grim Reaper with my healing in the process, is a good day at the office. Even with superpowers, I can't take all the credit. Those local heroes, the

mortal ones, they help humanity bounce back just as much as me

when disaster hits. The human spirit would give iron or diamonds

a run for their money when it came to sheer durability. Times like

these proved it.

Once I finished in San Francisco, I had one last task to

complete before returning to the ISS and fixing the stabilizer panel

that had served as a patch-donor.

The sinkhole off the coast of Japan was not going to close

itself off. I knew how to do it, but so many people were going to

be angry with me for a long time. Ah, the price of doing the right

thing.

In a fraction of a fraction of a second, I was hovering at the

base of El Capitan, a 3000-foot-tall, mile and a half wide piece of

solid granite dominating the horizon of Yosemite National Park, in

California. I carefully removed a few confused hikers and some surprised critters living there, feeling like a vandal for what I was about to do.

Being solid granite, it only took several solidly placed superhero-level punches at the base of the magnificent monolith to create a fissure spanning its entire length and width. Then, much like I did on Nea Kameni, I created a tunnel that positioned me directly beneath what I assumed to be the center of the behemoth. Once there, I lifted it and flew off with it balanced on my mortal-sized shoulders, leaving a crater in its place that would soon be the source of as much wonder as the mountain that once stood there.

To the observer, the sight of the enormous piece of granite flying west and heading out over the ocean must have been breathtaking at best, terrifying at worst. I would have been no more than a pimple on a whale's butt in comparison, so it probably appeared to be flying on its own.

Once over the ocean, and clear of traditional shipping lanes, I cranked up the speed. The beast I carried was pure granite. Aside from loose trees, rocks, and other assorted debris, there was little risk of my payload disintegrating from simple friction.

Several minutes later, I arrived at the sinkhole. Like a chef making pancakes on a skillet, I tossed El Capitan into the air, flipping it upside down as I did so. I caught the massive body, and in a single motion, I descended into the mouth of Charybdis, using El Capitan to plug the beast forever.

For the third time that day, I had to dig myself out through more than a mile and over a hundred thousand tons of stone. When I finally surfaced, I noticed an unexpected site. The second island I'd created in a day. Would they name it after me? Golden Sentinel Island had a nice ring to it, since Sentinel Island already existed. Oh, that would be 'Kogane no Hoshō no Shima', in Japanese, or 'Hwang-Geum Bochoui Seom', in Korean. Or maybe the United States would claim it as a U.S.

territory, seeing as I technically stole it from American soil, and it now sat in international waters.

Hey, I'm a superhero, not a diplomat.

I was just taking a deep breath when I heard yet another distress call. Seems a large apartment complex was on fire in the Detroit area. Yep, Detroit. Did I forget to mention I have reeeeeeeaaaaly good hearing too? Anyway, the firefighters were having a devil of a time containing the five-alarm mini-cataclysm.

A hero's work is never done.

7

Animehem: The Quest

Okay, my life's really weird. I'm the first to admit I'm not the most normal kid. I'm not a superhero or anything quite that cool, but I do know several.

Let's see. There's Pharaoh, Cool, Scalar, Hex, Yin-Yang, Dirk Claymore of the Clan McJagger, Santa Claus, and, um, Steve.

Pharaoh and Cool are a part of a superhero team called The Evolutants. Pharaoh, also called the Prince of Beasts, is a hyper-evolved lion with dreadlocks for a mane. He's wicked strong and built like Arnold Schwarzenegger – if Arnold was a lion who walked upright, wore denim coveralls, and spoke like a Rastafarian. That makes sense, right? Cool is an elastic giraffe. When I say elastic, I mean that dude can stretch high enough to high-five a 747! Yeah, that would be dangerous. It would probably frighten the passengers too. Like, who wouldn't be scared if some cartoon-looking giraffe with a huge Crest toothpaste grin and big shiny horsesh- um, giraffeshoes? Is that a thing? You know, tried to high-five their plane midflight? He's impressionable, so I won't suggest it. Cool is hyper-evolved, too. Aside from stretching, he can shape-shift. He's great at it. I've seen him impersonate Elvis, Mr. Rogers, Bob Ross, Batman – the '60s version, he even does the funny little vogue dance, and a hundred different animals! It's amazing, provided you can get past the fact that he's always yellow with brown spots. Every person, every animal, yellow with brown spots. I will say, a yellow T. rex with brown spots is still freaking terrifying. And he's *scary* good at the T. rex thing.

Scalar is also a man-beast sort of dude. He's a Dwayne Johnson-sized Minotaur, but with the head of a bison instead of a bull. Unlike Pharaoh and Cool, he wasn't hyper-evolved. He's a human prince, but an evil shaman cursed him more than a thousand years ago for falling in love with the wrong woman. He and Pharaoh have an odd relationship. Not really a bromance, more like some weird high school rivalry. They're constantly flexing on each other. Honestly, Pharaoh's stronger, but Scalar's a natural-born warrior. If they ever really threw down, it would be like the Punisher vs. John Wick. Pop some popcorn and pick a side because it's anybody's game!

Hex is a dinosaur from another superhero team called Team-Rex. She's a Tyrannosaurus-Hex if I understand correctly. Basically, she's a teenage Tyrannosaur who's also a witch. She's also kind of a b- um, blunt speaker. Oddly, her accent makes her sound like she's from somewhere in New England. Not exactly New York, more like Boston. 'Pahk the cah in Hahvid Yahd.' You know?

Hex is an odd bird, but she's, um, how would she put it? Wikkid powaful. Her feet rarely touch the ground, since she prefers to hover or fly, she can control lightning with her bare hands, make herself and other things invisible, control minds — she calls it *chahming*, and even bring dead plants back to life. Unfortunately, you can't reanimate animals. The brain activity becomes an issue. Brain death is forever unless you're lucky enough to have a backup of the patient's brain handy. But come on, this is the real world we're talking about, right?

Fun fact about Hex: her dead grandmother's spirit follows her everywhere she goes. A time travel experiment gone wrong sucked them both through a tem-portal, and now they're constantly together. Sounds awkward to me, but whatever. I thought she was nuts at first, hearing her talk to her grandmother like she was there with us. Only she can see or hear her. Who knows? Maybe she really *is* nuts.

Did I mention we're on a quest? It's wild. I feel like that little guy with the Robin Hood hat in the old Zelda game. "Take this sword, 'cause shit's about to get real!" And good god, did I ever get a sword! It's called the Sword of Helianthus. The deity of heat and light, Helianthus, blessed the sword, so great job naming it after him. The hilt looks like gold, but unlike everybody's

favorite wedding ring material, it's lightweight and stronger than

steel. The crest of Helianthus is engraved on the quillon block —

that's the crosspiece where the blade meets the handle. It's like a

flaming sunflower with a Freemason-looking eye at the center. I'm

generally not into flowery crap, but truth be told, it's pretty

badass. I have a chain-mail tee-shirt with a glowing key woven

into the chest, a black leather jacket and leather biker pants, a

magical water-skin that never goes dry, and black leather boots of

levitation. Gotta keep the ensemble consistent, right?

King Solidago Altissima tasked us with the quest. He

wasn't there personally, but Aconitum, his magic advisor, wizard,

warlock, whatever you want to call him, was there.

Aconitum was a creepy dude, to say the least. He wore a

drab brown robe that concealed most of his face with a monk's

hood and was the perfect blend of all the classic villain tropes. His

eyes were the color of ash burrowed in deep, leathery sockets, like twin tarantulas lurking in tunnels of flesh-colored webbing. He sported a long wizard hat of a schnoz, ending in a point that would've made Pinocchio do a double take. A set of thin, deflated lips that looked like a cocoon after the butterfly flew away framed his sullen mouth. Stringy, graying hair as clean as an old bicycle chain hung loosely around his pale, ghoulish face. His hands were so gnarled, laying them flat appeared to be an impossible task. That was alright because he seemed perfectly content to wring them together repeatedly in classic villain fashion whenever he spoke. His old, leather sandals betrayed filthy, calloused feet ending in long, jagged toenails. When he sneered – smiling obviously wasn't something Aconitum's face was accustomed to – it was painfully clear his dental hygiene was worse than his foot care routine. You'd think a wizard could use a little magic to tidy himself up a bit.

Our benefactor found my friends and me celebrating a recent victory at our longstanding tavern of choice, a tiny hole in the wall in the rough and tumble mining village of Artemisia, called

The Prancing Peony. Dirk, who happens to be an honest-to-God

ninja, was drinking blue agave tequila from one of Scalar's boots.

It's a long story that ends with something like a bad punchline.

You really don't want to hear it. Anyway, Dirk's full name is Dirk

Claymore McJagger *of the Clan McJagger.* Yep, he's as Scottish as

Highlands, golf courses, and kilts. His outfit is a sublimely strange

blend of Highlander warrior meets ninja. He wears a kilt, wee

black ninja booties, and the traditional black pajama top. His hair

and beard are a shade of red that, well… Let's put it this way, he's

basically Hagrid if he was a Weasley. In my opinion, he's too loud

to be a ninja. He carries an old claymore broadsword instead of a

katana. He also carries nunchucks. They're actually a couple of

lengths of tree trunk connected by an anchor chain, but they do

the trick. His magical bagpipes would blow your freakin' mind.

They're made from a dragon's bladder, and alicorns. Those are

unicorn horns in case you didn't know. They sound like Sir Sean

Connery after a few tankards of ale. Rest in peace, Sir Connery.

Other than their ability to speak, I haven't been able to figure out what's particularly magical about them. When I say them, I mean him. His name is Angus. Not that talking bagpipes aren't freaking magical, but Angus seems to be more of a hindrance than help most of the time. Ninjas are supposed to be stealthy, but whenever Dirk's sneaking around, Angus either complains like a Scottish C3-P0, or breathes loudly, which sounds like Scalar farting with a harmonica shoved in his butt. *Please don't ask how I know what that sounds like.*

Oh, wow! Dirk, Aconitum, quest. Yeah, I squirreled there, didn't I?

The quest! Dirk was drinking from Scalar's boot when Aconitum showed up, looking around the room like a frog at a fly convention. Pharaoh noticed him right away. I could see something was up, so I pulled him aside.

"Everything okay," I asked casually, trying not to be obvious.

Pharaoh raised a bushy eyebrow and nodded in Aconitum's direction. "Dat mon smell bad."

"Maybe he's in a grunge band," I asked. "He looks old enough."

Pharaoh isn't exactly quick on the draw when it comes to humor. He's not unintelligent, but his wit is dryer than Arizona in the summer. "Nuh. Me mean he smell like a bad mon."

I nodded. "Yeah, he looks like he's up to no good." We watched him through the usual crowd of Friday night patrons, a volatile mixture of miners, farmers, vagabonds, and thieves. "Wanna see what he's up to," I asked.

Before Pharaoh could respond, Hex floated towards the cloaked man and blocked our view. "Wah she doing," Pharaoh wondered, even though she was clearly talking to Aconitum.

~

Fewer than half our party gathered on either side of a long wooden table near the center of the room. Hex was at the bar when Aconitum slunk through the door. Yin-Yang was playing darts with Cool in a dimly lit corner. Santa and Steve were hustling some farmers at a card game known as Black-Eyed Susan.

Dirk and Scalar threw back shots of some God-awful smelling alcohol. Pharaoh and I, as inconspicuously as possible, stared at the back of Hex's head. We watched for several minutes, waiting for some indication as to where the conversation might be leading. Our patience was rewarded moments later when Hex turned in midair, causing us to avert our gazes guiltily, and brought the conversation directly to our table.

"Suh, how bout di weather," Pharaoh commented a little too nonchalantly.

"You two can give up the innocent act," Hex muttered. "I've told you before-"

"Yeah, we know," I interrupted. "Eyes in the back of your head."

Pharaoh adjusted his seat while Hex and Aconitum sat down across from us, ignoring Dirk and Scalar's drunken hijinks.

Hex motioned towards her new friend, who hungrily eyed an untouched platter of fried quaker ladies. "Aconitum is here on behalf of King Solidago Altissima. He's searching for champions to rescue the king's son from an evil coven of witches known as Noisetier des Sorcières. There's a substantial reward, and he'll provide us with gear and a map to guide us."

"Why doesn't the king just send his knights to rescue his son," I asked. To Aconitum, who was still eying the quaker ladies, I said, "Dig in if you're hungry."

The warlock pulled the bounty towards him and began to devour the platter's contents, pausing only to summon Viola, the barmaid, to the table. "Ale," he ordered through a full mouth. "Tankard!" As she scuttled off to fulfill his request, he

shouted, "On their tab!" He motioned around the table with a wild

sweeping gesture, and then went back to stuffing his face.

Hex stared at him for a moment, clearly disgusted, but

continued. "The queen doesn't know her son is missing, and the

king wants to keep it that way. Sending the king's guard on such

a quest would prompt the queen to ask questions the king would

rather not answer."

I knew better than to ask Aconitum, who hadn't spoken to

anyone other than Hex and Viola, any further questions about the

king or the circumstances of the prince's assumed abduction. The

king was a private man. Questions made him less than comfortable.

Nobody in their right mind made the king less than comfortable.

I looked at Pharaoh, who nodded thoughtfully. "Alright,

Hex. You've got our attention. Go on."

~

Hex's tail was long, but her tale was short. Get it? Tail? Tale? Oh, God, I'm turning into my dad. Scratch that first line. Forget I said any of it, please.

Hex's story was a short one, but it was so full of intrigue and betrayal, it could have been a Shakespearean play, or a Mexican soap opera.

Solidago Altissima's kingdom, the once lovely Candytuft, was in all sorts of agricultural distress. He turned to a coven of witches to resolve his problems. That's like going to a loan shark to resolve financial troubles, or a crossroads demon for like... anything. The piper always demands payment in the end.

The king apparently made a deal with the twelve witches and their silent partner. Once the witches solved his problems with magic, he arrested them for practicing witchcraft instead of paying up. I'm still not clear on what the agreed payment was. Dick move, if you ask me. All attempts to incarcerate the witches obviously failed, and you can probably guess how the rest went

127

down. Not only did the crops start dying again, but the king's only son, Prince Ranunculus Goldenrod, vanished as he slept one night. Thirteen deadly flowers were left on his pillow, a clear message as to who took him, and of their intent.

Apparently, the king discovered the flowers. He told Queen Ursinia that their son went on a hunting expedition with Sir Scabiosa Atropurpurea and would be gone for several days. It had been two days since the prince's abduction. With each passing day, the king knew the likelihood of ever seeing his son alive again grew increasingly unlikely.

Atropurpurea, also known as the Black Knight, or Blackamoor's Beauty to the village maidens, camped out in the swamplands to the south of Candytuft. No one but knights hunting goblins or ogres dared set foot in the swamp, let alone spent a night or more, but there the Black Knight remained, faithfully awaiting word from Aconitum. He would lead whatever party was brave, or perhaps foolish enough, to accept the warlock's proposal.

Hex finished her story with a sideways glance at the warlock. Absolutely no one could compete with her level of stink-eye. She was the grand master of the craft. "Would you say that was an accurate retelling of your proposal?" Her words dripped more sarcasm than Aconitum dripped drool and God knew what else.

The warlock nodded and involuntarily gagged while mumbling, which ended up sounding something like a cat hacking up a hairball. He was a class act all the way. I had a hard time imagining him in the king's court.

Hex shook her head ruefully. "So, what do you think? I'm in if you are."

I looked at Pharaoh, his brows furrowed in deep thought. "What say you, big guy," I asked.

"Nuh. I tink we should aks di others," he mused.

I looked around the room at the others. "Dude, Scalar and Dirk aren't in any condition to make decisions, but they're always ready for a fight. There's a reward involved, so Santa and Steve will be in. There's a child in danger, so Yin-Yang would go regardless of the reward, and Cool would follow you into the twisting depths of Pothos itself. I'd say the three of us can safely make the call."

Pharaoh shook his head, his dreadlocks swaying disapprovingly. "Nuh mon. We do dis how we always do it. Wit a vote."

I sighed. Pharaoh was a rules guy through and through. There would be no getting around his lawful good nature. "Fine," I said after a moment's consideration. "Hey, Scalar, Dirk!"

The two turned to look at us, bleary-eyed.

"How would you feel about a quest? We'd get to rescue a little boy!"

They stared at us, processing what they'd heard.

"There's a reward," I continued.

Still no response. The pair's eyes were glazed over like bloodshot donut holes.

"And fighting," I added.

"Oh, aye, a quest would be just GRAND!" Dirk interrupted, throwing his hands in the air, inadvertently tossing his drink into Scalar's eyes.

Barely fazed, Scalar picked up a dirty bar towel that was cleaner than his face and sopped off the drink before nodding. "Si compadre. A quest." He seemed ready to say something profound, his eyes taking on a somber cast. "Sure. Why not?"

I turned to Pharaoh triumphantly. "There you have it! Five of nine in favor of the quest. Majority rules, yes?"

Pharaoh narrowed his eyes, looking like Santa and Steve just cheated him at Black-Eyed Susan. "Yuh pull dis crap every time. An me always let yuh git away wit it." He finally shook his head and shrugged. "Fine. We go rescue di prince. But nuh blame me when dem witches turn yuh inta a toad."

Dirk turned, a twinkle in his bloodshot eyes. "Have ye laddies ever tried frog's legs? Almost as yummy as haggis, they are!"

~

We waited a few hours for Dirk and Scalar to sober up, listening to Angus complain about Dirk's clear intolerance of alcohol. The evening finally ended in a short-lived bar fight with the farmers whom Santa and Steve had apparently cleaned out of every last pachira. Pharaoh ended the fight by buying the farmers

drinks, and sending them home happy, still broke, but happy.

Yin-Yang and Cool returned to the table shortly after we

made the decision to go on the quest. Cool, as always, was

agreeable to whatever Pharaoh thought was best. However, Yin-

Yang, the quintessential Gemini, wanted to look at everything from

both sides before committing.

Yin-Yang was typically at odds with everything, including

himself. When I say him, I mean them. Yin and Yang, a pair of

bears whose actual breed I didn't know, were fraternal

twins. They were nearly identical twins, but Yin was as black as

pitch, and Yang was as white as newly fallen snow. Yin was a cleric

and had mastered the ability to control and blend into

shadows. He couldn't create complete darkness, but he came

damned close. Yang, on the other hand, was a monk who could

create spiritual lights so bright they could turn your retinas into

tiny charcoal briquettes. He, like his brother and his shadows, could become invisible in the midst of his self-generated light. Most surprising was the fact that his light, no matter how bright, generated absolutely zero heat.

Yin and Yang's third power, or second to each of them I guess, was to combine their body mass to become a much larger black and white bear closely resembling a Giant Panda.

In addition to their mystical abilities, the pair was as stealthy as Dirk believed himself to be. They, like one of Santa's farts, were silent *and* deadly. Individually, they were dangerous enough, but when they worked as one, they were a powerful force to be reckoned with. There's some life lesson in there, but I'm telling a story here, not expounding philosophical insights.

Yin-Yang had one clear weakness. As balanced as his powers were in his combined form, he was a bit indecisive. Left, right, up, down, war, peace. There was always a brief internal debate. Yin and Yang were, for all intents and purposes, polar opposites. I'm doing my best to avoid the obvious polar bear joke.

Generally, whatever direction had the moral or ethical high ground, was the direction he gravitated to. Thankfully, both of their respective orders served Helianthus. I can't imagine the turmoil serving two gods would create.

Yin-Yang sat quietly at our table, meditating as Angus berated Dirk for not having the fortitude of a dragon's bladder, which, if I understand correctly, can handle alcohol better than any other living being. Considering it's the liver that processes alcohol, I'm pretty sure Angus is full of crap. Dirk's the only one obstinate enough to actually carry on a debate with Angus, so I let them banter.

The bear, bears, you know… finally agreed the rescue of a young prince was worth the risks a quest imposed. Deeply nodding with hands together in praise, he was in.

Santa and Steve, as I predicted, were automatically in for the loot. Once Scalar and Dirk were sober enough to travel, we made our way to the swamplands of Capitula. Aconitum of course, led the way.

~

For as much as Aconitum looked like he would blow apart if you sneezed too hard around him, he was spry. The dude moved like a teenage boy on prom night. I guessed he had a vested interest in getting the prince back in one piece because he was all about getting us on our way.

Artemisia is a small mining town on the southern coast of Capitula. Though the distance to Sir Scabiosa Atropurpurea's encampment was only about seven SLAs — a Specific Leaf Area is about half a mile — navigating the perils of the swamp took several hours. In addition to the poisonous laurentiis and the man-eating kalanchoes, there were ogres and goblins to contend with. Thankfully, the goblins are cowards, and generally shy away from parties as large as ours. The ogres, however, are ill-tempered pack hunters. Our little band of nine, ten if you counted

Aconitum, eleven if you counted Yin-Yang twice, was still a fair target.

We never saw any ogres either.

Just kidding.

We'd just entered a small clearing, about a half an SLA from Sir Scabby's camp, when we found ourselves surrounded by a nasty looking ogre horde. There were more than twenty of the brutes, each carrying an uprooted tree as a club, and standing least a foot taller than Pharaoh. I'm surprised none of us smelled them before entering the clearing, especially Pharaoh. One of the ogres, the shortest of the crew, though built like a grain silo, began shouting. I'm assuming he was shouting at the other ogres because he was speaking Jogishkis, the regional ogre dialect.

"Anyone speak ogre," I asked, just loud enough for my group to hear.

"He said to kill the skinny ones first, capture the strong ones for labor, and save the fat one and the child to eat at tonight's feast." Santa laughed jovially, patting his belly. Then he patted Steve on the head and laughed even louder. *"Child."*

"Ho ho ho," Steve muttered sarcastically. Though Hex was the undisputed reigning champion of the sarcasm game, her eye rolls alone earning her legendary status, he was nearly her equal.

Santa – yep, the *real* Santa Claus – was clearly not intimidated by the ogre's desire to feast on him and Steve. Steve, on the other hand, seemed uncomfortable with the idea. Maybe he was just irritated at being called a child. Steve was somewhere in the neighborhood of seven hundred years old. While he didn't look particularly young to us, to a giant being like an ogre, he probably looked like a child when compared to the rest of our party.

Santa, while not as physically imposing as Pharaoh or Scalar, or as skilled a fighter as Dirk or Yin-Yang, was still a force to be reckoned with. He was a big man, to say the least, and not just his girth. He was heavily bearded, physically hearty, and carried himself like one of the ancient Norse gods. His laugh could turn the tide of most disagreements, and being a druid, he had some magical abilities that were almost on par with Hex's. With a touch of his nose, he could transform himself into a column of red smoke that looked like a lit emergency flare. In his smoke form, he could induce coughing spasms in his foes, pass through small spaces, like keyholes, under doors, and yes, even down chimneys. He could see auras, which was useful when determining whether someone was bad or good. And he had this uncanny ability to know whether the enemy was asleep or awake. In addition to his innate magical abilities, he also had an enchanted sack of carrying and an endless supply of coal. He could even enchant reindeer to fly, which would have been super useful if there were reindeer in Capitula. Santa was as formidable a hero as any I traveled with.

Fun and slightly embarrassing fact about everyone's favorite saint: Santa almost exclusively orders milk and cookies at The Prancing Peony. Dirk makes fun of him, but always steals a cookie or two when Santa's not looking. Unfortunately, Santa is extremely lactose intolerant. Any form of dairy gives him explosive gas that could power a blacksmith's kiln.

Steve, as I might have mentioned before, is an elf. Don't call him an elf, he hates that. He's actually an E.L.V.E. Technically he's an elf too, but E.L.V.E. stands for Elite Lethal Villain Exterminator, which frankly sounds much more badass.

Steve's one of the best in the biz. Don't let his size fool you. His fighting skills are on a level that rivals Hex's level of sarcasm. Even Scalar, the one thousand-year-old warrior, can't match Steve's moves. If anyone could keep up with him, they might invent a new martial art called Steve.

Steve didn't even wait for anyone to try and talk to the ogres first. At the first sign of aggression, he vanished behind

Santa, which of course caused the ogres to laugh almost as hard as Santa, who, knowing what was about to happen, laughed harder still. A moment later, Steve emerged with two unsheathed daggers that looked like swords in his tiny hands. The next fifteen to twenty seconds were little more than a blur. The E.L.V.E. literally leapt from ogre to ogre, slicing throats and jamming his daggers up through the armpits of the surprised giants, piercing their enormous hearts.

The ogres dropped like dominoes. As Steve approached the final, unfortunate ogre, Dirk leapt forward and shrieked, "The last one is mine, laddie!"

Dirk's longsword cut an arc through the air, whistling as it separated the last ogre's head from its hulking shoulders. The monster's final expression was utter surprise and confusion as it rolled out of the clearing.

A moment later, a knight dressed in the finest armor any of us had ever laid eyes on, walked into the clearing holding the ogre's massive head under one of his arms. He nodded curtly at Aconitum. He didn't appear to be a fan of the warlock.

"Well, my good fellows," he began, smiling as he looked us over. To Hex he added, "And milady. My name is Sir Scabiosa Atropurpurea, knight of his majesty King Solidago Altissima's royal court and commander of the royal guard. But you, my friends, may call me Atro."

~

Atro, it seemed, was a real knight's knight. According to the legends, he was regular old Sir Galahad. Or maybe Sir Galahad was a regular old Sir Scabby? Does it really matter? He was a genuinely good dude. The king chose him to command the royal guard for many reasons, bravery and chivalry being the basest of them. Not to mention, he looked dashing as hell in his armor, like he was born to be a knight. Even Hex, who was pretty well immune to all men's charms, seemed to be the tiniest bit taken by him as he spoke. She might even go as far as to say he was chahming.

Our newest companion invited us back to his camp, where he casually tossed the ogre's head onto an impressive pile of laurentii and kalanchoe hides, as well as a few additional ogre heads and a fresh goblin corpse. Sir Scabby had been busy while he waited for Aconitum to return to the camp with a party worthy of his quest. Clearly he was capable of handling things pretty well on his own, which made me wonder about what awaited us on our quest ahead, and if he actually needed us.

Sir Scabby's camp was too small to fit all of us comfortably, so most of us found a spot among the trees on the perimeter of the tiny encampment, well within earshot of the bold knight.

"Within this wall of flesh, brave ones, there is a soul that in all sincerity counts thee its creditor for joining this dangerous mission. Aye, 'tis true that some of us may not returneth from what may very well be'est a suicide mission, but rest assured I wilt lay down mine life for any or all of thee. The young prince must be'est rescued. Each of thee is now mine brother, and sister, in arms. We share a common goal, and together, we wilt accomplish the otherwise impossible." He stopped and raised a cup to us. The receptacle was empty, of course, as our new friend had no spirits on the premises. He was there to save the prince, not get drunk.

Jeez, how could you not believe in him? He was a regular old Captain America. Well, more like Captain Capitula. That has a nice ring to it. Sorry, squirreling again. After his rousing speech, he stood and popped the lid off a crudely manufactured crate he'd been sitting on and began taking out items wrapped in some sort of woven burlap. His exodus from the castle had clearly been covert. He brought few supplies, so as not to raise any suspicions in the queen or any of her servants or advisors.

He shook his head ruefully as he began sorting through the wrapped packages. "Thither art more of thee than I hadst planned for. I most sorrowfully regret I didst not bringeth enough weapons for each of thee."

Dirk stepped forward, drawing his longsword with his right hand, and clutching his dagger in his left. "Worry not laddie. I never leave home without mi'blades!"

Steve held up his massive daggers. Congealing ogre's blood dripped lazily onto his hands. "No need here, either," he agreed gruffly.

Cool held up his two forefeet and fashioned a series of weapons between them. He shifted from a club to a sword, to a mace, and so forth, before finishing by connecting them and forming a large, seamless, polished shield. "I make my weapons as I need 'em, bro!"

Even Hex, who seemed to hang on each of Captain Capitula's fancy words, held up her magical staff with a smirk. "My magic is my weapon."

Finally, Pharaoh held up his clenched fists. "Me need nutten more dan dees, mon," he said without an ounce of arrogance. He was right. His fists were the veritable hammers of the gods.

Sir Scabby smiled. The revelation pleased him. "Well then, t'appeareth I shalt has't enough weapons after all."

~

The first package Sir Scabby unrolled was a set of axes. More accurately, it was a huge double-bladed battleaxe and a pair of wicked looking hatchets. He looked at the remaining members of our party, and finally passed the bundle to Scalar, who was beyond pleased with the gift. Scalar was quite polite when he wasn't drunk. He offered a slight bow. His bow wasn't of the deep and rigid nature you might see in many Asian cultures. It was a short dip of the head and shoulders, his face still fixed on his benefactor, as old-school European noblemen would do.

Sir Scabby matched the nod, and then returned to the contents of the crate.

Next was a massive war-hammer with a huge flat surface on one end of the head and an eight-inch spike on the other. The leather-wrapped handle appeared iron-forged, adorned with huge, flawless diamonds, rubies, and emeralds. The colors of Christmas. It was no mistake, of course, when Atro offered the hammer to Santa, who accepted it graciously, and immediately began testing its weight and balance.

"Watch where you swing that thing," Steve growled. "Save your aggression for the ogres."

Santa, always the good sport, laughed heartily and patted Steve on the head. "Oh, don't be such a party pooper, Steve. Besides, shouldn't you be cleaning your daggers?"

Steve glanced up at his huge companion. Their size difference reminded me of a rhino and an oxpecker, the little bird that sits on the rhino's back and cleans its ears. I kept my personal observation just that, personal. I didn't want my head joining the pile at the edge of the clearing. "I like them bloody," Steve muttered. "Lets my prey know I mean business."

Santa leaned on the tree nearest to him and raised his hands slightly in mock surrender. "I can see how that would be effective."

"Damn right." Steve nodded.

Sir Scabby had already returned to the crate when the exchange ended. He pulled out a long wooden bo staff and handed it to the quiet and contemplative Yin-Yang. The panda-ish bear's bow was deep and solemn. Amazingly, Sir Scabby matched it perfectly, which couldn't have been easy in all his armor.

Finally, he pulled two smaller burlap-wrapped packages out of the crate and looked at me. "T'appeareth I shalt has't one to spare," he conceded happily.

Yin-Yang cleared his throat lightly before stepping apart and becoming his twin selves.

Sir Scabby grinned. "Well now, isn't that a clever trick?" He looked at the two packages carefully, weighing options in his head before handing one of them to Yin, as Yang held the bo staff.

Yin unwrapped the package gingerly. Something clinked within its folds. He let the burlap drop at his feet, exposing a lethal looking chained morningstar. The handle was more than a foot long, connected to a fist-sized ball of spiked iron by a chain about eight inches in length. There was a leather strap at the end of the handle, so Yin slipped his hand through. He was pleased with the gift, as his second bow in as many minutes indicated.

Sir Scabby bowed back again, not even the slightest shudder was visible, though the weight of his armor should have made a bow that deep and prolonged nearly impossible. Dude must have had an insane core workout routine.

The knight then turned his attention back to me. "The final item in this small arsenal cometh from mine own personal collection. T'attunes well to creative spirits. I sense thee art one of the finest bards in this land."

For someone who tends to have a lot to say, I found myself speechless.

Cool finally clapped me on the back with one of his massive hooves, and declared, "He does weave a pretty exciting yarn, bruh!"

Sir Scabby nodded. "I receiveth a feeleth for these things. Akin to aura readings, but more of a quiet instinct than a bold vision." He handed me my package. If you were paying attention earlier, then you know what was in it.

The mighty Sword of Helianthus.

8

Animehem: Round Two
Are You *Sure* You Want to Do This?

Once the gift-giving was over, Sir Scabby took the burlap that had covered our new weapons and draped the pieces in a crisscrossed formation over the pile of heads and hides at the edge of his camp. He then broke down the wooden crate and built what looked like a teepee over the pile. After packing away or piling up any evidence he'd ever been there he took a flint out of one of the half dozen pouches at his waist. With a few well-placed sparks, he had an impressive, if not foul-smelling fire raging.

"Won't that attract unwanted attention, my lord," Aconitum asked, appearing chaotic-nervous.

"Better the attention beest hither, than whither we're headed," Sir Scabby replied. "And unless thou art joining us, thee should be'est returning to the castle, post-haste."

The warlock offered a facial expression that looked like a kalanchoe stalking its prey, yet I'm pretty sure it was meant to be a smile. He should seriously stick to frowning or poker faces. "As you say, my lord." Turning to the rest of us, he said, "You'll get what's coming to you when you return with the prince, unharmed." That completely not creepy, non-foreshadowy speech given, he darted off into the woods like the filthy, crazed murder-hobo I suspected him to be.

Cool, as innocent as a newborn baby, laughed as Aconitum scurried off like a rat into a maze. "Heh. He was nice, but he could use a bath. And a toothbrush. Maybe a pedicure, too. Hey, when we get our rewards, we should all chip in and get him a gift certificate for the kingdom day spa!"

Scalar hefted his huge axe over his shoulder and hung it across his back. He'd fashioned one of the kalanchoe hides into a makeshift bandoleer. He used an additional hide to make twin axe-holsters, which hung loosely from his belt, one on each hip. Scalar was handy with the hides, that was for sure. "Please, Cool, my dear friend, take no offense when I say, *hell no.* That stinky culo is the king's advisor. If he wishes to spend a day cleansing his body to make himself look and smell like a respectable creature, then I am quite sure the king would be happy to accommodate him."

Sir Scabby laughed heartily at Scalar's response, giving one of Santa's guffaws a run for its money. "Friend Minotaur, thee feeleth as most of the kingdom doth feel. T'is a mystery wherefore the king alloweth Aconitum to remain at his side. His loyalty and motives has't at each moment been in question amongst the knights of the royal court."

Cool snaked his head around the trees, his neck winding like a creeping laurentii, and whispered into Sir Scabby's ear. "He's not a Minotaur, dude. He's a cursed prince. He just looks like a Minotaur."

Both Cool and the knight glanced back at Scalar, the revelation burning between them. Sir Scabby whispered back. "Forsooth he doest. I shalt be'est more careful in the days to come."

Scalar snorted and plodded into the woods to await directions and grumbled. "I can hear you whispering."

~

The witches' lair, cave, tent, teepee, whatever they lived in, was in a region north of what we'd always considered north. Like, so far north, no one from Capitula ever ventured there. It was, as it turned out, beyond the land of the dragons, a place no one ever returned from. We, in our haste, um, my haste actually, agreed to go. Pharaoh offered more than one 'I told you so' or in his case, 'Me did tell yuh suh', as we made our way into the lands to the west of Candytuft.

We'd briefly considered going directly through Candytuft, but the risk of the queen, or one of her many handmaidens or advisors, seeing Sir Scabby was too great. We chose to circumvent the castle, and everything in its vicinity, by taking the western route.

I know what you're thinking. *What? The western trail? Are you out of your mind?*

And yes, you're right, taking the western trail *was* going to be dangerous. But think about it. Facing trolls, orcs, and creeping shadows in the western forests would be far less problematic than battling gnomes, ghouls, and golems in the rocky crags that made up Capitula's eastern borderlands. The eastern route was nothing short of suicide. Not that everything in the northern territories wouldn't be trying to kill us the moment we arrived, but the western route gave us a better chance of getting there in one piece.

The group was glum, even by our standards. Only Sir Scabby seemed to have a modicum of confidence that we might survive our quest. Dirk and Scalar moped along like children sent out to shovel snow, while Santa and Steve brought up the rear, whispering, so the horrors lurking around the swamp couldn't hear. Hex floated along at the head of the group, keeping pace with Sir Scabby. Pharaoh, Yin, and Yang bravely took the left and right flanks. Even Cool was uncharacteristically quiet, plodding along thoughtfully, occasionally laughing at a joke only he could hear.

I got the impression nobody wanted to walk with me, as I was given a wide berth at the middle of the group. I felt like a soap-covered finger at the center of a glass of peppered water. If I moved closer, they moved farther away.

And was that a giggle I heard in Angus's ever-present wheeze?

Screw 'em. I didn't want to talk to any of them anyway.

~

Have I mentioned how much I hate swamps? Soggy boots are the freaking worst. And leeches? They get into your pants, and-

Yeah, don't get me started. The only thing I hate more than the leeches, ogres, and goblins that seemed to like living in that mucking place, are the arachnodactyls. Because how do you make hairy, wolf-sized spiders even more terrifying? Give 'em effing wings, that's how! Those damned things seemed to be happy living anywhere with deep shadow banks and plenty of food. There's plenty of food in the swamp because they'll eat anything that has a soft, chewy center. I'm like a big, delicious wonton to those bastards.

Swamp-serpents, laurentiis, kalanchoes, and spine-toothed jawfish filled the murky brown swamp-waters. I'm sure I'm forgetting a few things, but you get the picture.

On a normal day, a walk from Lake Billy Buttons to the northern farmlands of Candytuft took slightly over a half a day. Turn the trek into a semicircle around the kingdom, and the ETA more than doubled. Add the time it would take to traverse the northern mountains, all while hiding from hungry dragons? We were in for a three-day hike, at least. Hell, we didn't know how far beyond the mountains our quarry was, or what horrors lived in the lands north of the dragons.

We were in deep shit.

The path narrowed up ahead, and the team began to draw into a single file. The swamp rose on both sides of the trail, giving us little more than a 2-foot-wide, muddy path to follow.

Dirk grumbled as one of his booties got sucked off his foot with a thick, wet slurp. He retrieved it and nonchalantly hung it from one of Scalar's horns. Ol' Tatanka Head didn't seem to notice, and I wasn't about to cause a skirmish out there in the swamp, so I kept my mouth shut.

Low-hanging willow branches covered with patches of moss and fungus drooped lazily ahead. We brushed them aside like a never-ending curtain of beads as we moved blindly forward.

Steve scurried ahead, passing deftly between our legs until he'd taken the lead. "I can see ahead," he called back. "The branches don't get in my way!"

"What do you see," Sir Scabby asked, trying to duck, but still having no luck.

"The path widens again in about a half an SLA. Twice that distance and we'll be out of the swamp," Steve replied. "The forest is dead ahead!"

"You had to say 'dead', didn't you," Hex muttered.

A shadow in the swamp water to my right drew my attention. I slowed my pace a bit, trying to follow its movement. Something was in the water, and it was moving fast. Too fast!

By the time I realized what I was seeing, it was already too late. It was a reflection! I looked up just in time to see a dozen arachnodactyls silently descending upon us in a frenzy. "Run," I shouted.

Before anyone could get clear of the willow branches, they were on us. Steve was the first to go. One of those damned winged monstrosities picked him up and dragged him, kicking and screaming, into the treetops. Next was Angus, as an overzealous arachnodactyl misjudged the difference between Dirk and his noisy friend.

Dirk shrieked, reaching into the air for his friend, but as with Steve, it was too late.

The next to go... *was me!*

One of the beasts grabbed my ankle and dragged me roughly to the ground. I drew my sword and rolled to strike at the bastard but was horrified to see it wasn't an arachnodactyl at all. Nope, it was one of those other things I'd forgotten about.

A long, leathery tentacle coiled around my leg, and dragged me into the swamp. I was waist deep before I could get enough balance to swing my sword. At that point, I risked taking off my own leg if I wasn't careful.

"Packard!" I heard a voice that could only be Pharaoh's cry out. A strong hand clamped onto my shoulder. I guess he wasn't that mad at me after all.

A moment later, I took in a mouthful of putrid water. Shortly after that, I blacked out.

LEVEL TWO
CHEAT CODES

9

Respawned

Pharaoh's grip seemed to loosen as I crawled back towards consciousness. The big lug was worried about me after all.

"Packard," someone said, sounding concerned. "Packard, can you hear me?"

It wasn't Pharaoh. Santa?

I opened my mouth, expecting to taste swamp water. Instead, I tasted an odd mixture of antiseptic and cinnamon. "Huh? Santa," I croaked.

"Well, I'll admit I haven't shaven for several days, but I'm not *that* shaggy."

I knew that voice. It wasn't anybody from my little team of adventurers. It was… "Dad?" I tried to open my eyes, but the light in the room was blinding in comparison to the hazy, filtered light of the swamp. I coughed. My throat was sore, and my muscles ached. "Dad? Is that you?"

I heard a sob, followed by a quick, embarrassed sniffle. "Yeah, son. It's me." He sobbed again before whispering, "How do, uh, how do you feel?"

I coughed again. "Like I was dragged into a swamp by the Eleventacles and drowned," I said finally. "I know that doesn't make any sense."

"Eleventacles," an unfamiliar woman's voice asked.

"Uh, they're like tentacles, but they go to eleven," my dad explained. "They're a pretty vicious monster in one of the games I developed." My dad's voice dropped as he continued. "Packard's mind is sorting things out, trying to make sense of everything."

"That's my last memory, dad," I cut in. "In fact, it's my only clear memory."

"But you know who you are, and who I am," dad countered. "That's good." He was quiet for a moment, except for the breathing through his nose. He always did that when he was thinking.

"Dad, what happened," I asked. "Why don't I remember anything? I mean, anything real. It's all stuff from the games, but only bits and pieces, like a partly built jigsaw puzzle." I looked around the room. My eyes were finally adjusting, and what I saw frightened me. I was in a hospital bed, but not in a hospital room. Complex looking equipment straight out of *Tom Mux: Space Marine* surrounded me. "Dad, am I still in a game?"

My dad looked startled. "Wha- No! Why would you think that?"

The woman stepped forward and placed a hand on dad's shoulder. There was a familiarity in the touch. Not in a creepy, sexy times way, but like someone who knew him and cared about what he was feeling. She looked conflicted. "Hal, he doesn't know. How could he?"

Dad turned abruptly. "I wanted to give him time," he snapped. My dad, the king of cool, snapped. "I wanted- I wanted..." He sighed. "Oh, Jesus, Packard, just relax for a little while, please. Things have happened. I want to explain. I *will* explain, I promise, but I need you to trust me. Can you do that?"

"Dad?" I was scared. "Wha- what happened?" I looked at the woman, but she had a better poker face than Santa. "Are you okay, dad? Am- am *I* okay?" I looked at the equipment. "I've gotten worse, haven't I?"

Dad shook his head. He looked distressed and that scared the hell out of me.

"Please, dad. Whatever it is, please tell me. Because you're really scaring me."

He sighed. "You, um, there was an accident. A bad one." Dad swallowed hard and straightened his shoulders. "We were broadsided on our way to work, son. My airbag deployed, so I walked away with a couple of bruises and a black eye. But the impact crumpled your door and your head slammed against the glass. You suffered severe head trauma, son."

"But I'm okay now, right? I feel like there's something else you're not telling me, dad." I was dizzy and getting nauseous, but I needed to know what was going on.

The woman nudged my dad. "He should know everything, Hal."

Hal turned again, angry. "Christ, would you just let me do this?"

The woman recoiled, clearly not used to seeing my dad act like that. She wasn't alone.

"Dad, please," I said.

My dad dropped his chin to his chest. He'd obviously been through hell, which scared me even more. What had happened to me?

"Dad, please!" I blurted again. "What happened to me?"

"You died, son." His breathing was shaky, like he was holding back more sobs. "They were able to resuscitate you, but when they did, you'd lost all brain function. You were brain-dead, Packard," he whispered. "You've been brain-dead for more than four months.

~

Okay. I'll admit, of all the things I was expecting to hear, machines keeping me alive for the last four months wasn't one of them.

"Dad, I thought we talked about that." I felt like I was going to throw up. "I had a signed DNR, dad. You agreed."

"I know, Packard," he said softly. "It was one thing agreeing to it, but doing it? Son..." He started to cry again. His breath came in hitches as he spoke. "I kept justifying keeping you alive because you didn't-"

"Die," I asked. "Because I didn't die the way you expected? Dad, that's just semantics! You're telling me I was brain-dead for four months, and you never once thought to honor my request?"

Dad was clearly trying to justify his actions, but I was so angry. I wanted to punch something, fly somewhere, scream, but as I considered my next words, my dad just dropped to his knees and sobbed.

"I think you should know everything," the woman standing with dad said. I'd honestly forgotten she was there.

"Who even are you," I asked her, maybe a bit too coarsely. I was frustrated, frightened, and sick to my stomach. Really, I didn't know if I wanted to be chatting it up with a stranger who just witnessed one of the most uncomfortable moments between my dad and me.

"You probably don't remember me," she said, placing a hand on dad's shoulder. "I'm Irene Chow. I've been a friend and colleague of your father's for almost 30 years. We went to college together, and I was at your parents' wedding. I met you once when you were about seven or eight. You showed my daughter, Lillian, how to find a secret room on one of your dad's old Atari games."

"Yeah, it was the game with the microdot. Then we all had peanut butter and jelly," I answered. "My mom made them because Lillian never got them at home."

"You remember that," she asked, eyes narrowed, betraying her surprise.

"Yeah. But that memory's fragmented too. I honestly can't tell you what memories are real and what was just a game." I looked from Irene to my father, and back again. Something was up, and Irene wanted to spill the beans. My stomach lurched. "Trash can!"

Irene quickly stepped away from my father's side and grabbed a trash can from beside the door. She handed it to me just in time.

What came up tasted a lot more like swamp water than the antiseptic and cinnamon I'd been tasting since waking up. And then came the dreaded dry heaves.

As I retched into the trash can, I could see Irene gently help dad into an uncomfortable looking plastic chair where he hunched over and sighed dejectedly. He was a broken man. I loved my dad, and I didn't mean to punish him for his decision. I just felt betrayed.

Irene returned and rubbed my back while I finished dry heaving.

"Water," she asked.

"Please," I replied hoarsely.

She retrieved a bottle of Divining Rod drinking water from a mini fridge with a glass door. I downed half the bottle before taking a deep breath.

"Thank you," I said softly.

Irene nodded, still contemplating her next words.

"Look, Irene, if you're willing to tell me what's going on, I'd really like to know. I mean, I think I deserve to know. Don't I?"

Irene nodded again. There was a quickness and decisiveness in her nod that told me she agreed. "How do I begin," she mused, mostly to herself.

I shrugged my shoulders. "At the beginning is usually good."

Thankfully, Irene's voice had an unusual calming effect to it, like a female Morgan Freeman narrating my poor life's choices with an odd touch of dignity. "Four months ago, you and your dad were on your way to the testing facility. I suppose it was like any other day. You'd stopped for an iced coffee and a doughnut. As you were pulling out of the drive-through, a wrong-way driver speeding north on Dolores jumped the curb and slammed into your door. Your dad was a little banged up, but you hit your head on the window, causing severe head trauma. Until a few minutes ago, you were brain-dead."

I knew it was rude, but I interrupted her anyway. "Dad already told me that. Are you telling me that's all there is? Why am I here, wherever here is, instead of in a hospital? Why can I feel my legs? And why am I so damned nauseous?"

Dad looked up, startled by something I said. It was probably the bit about me feeling my legs, as that hadn't been a thing for a long time. I wouldn't let his sudden interest distract me. I wanted Irene to tell me everything before he tried to shut her up again.

"You can feel your legs," Irene asked, looking more pleased than surprised. "That's good, Packard! *Excellent.*"

I nodded. "And? Why can I feel them? I should be worse, not better, right? There's more, and I deserve to know."

Irene looked back at dad, who'd reverted to his sad, pensive stare. "After the paramedics resuscitated you, they took you to the UC San Francisco Medical Center," Irene continued. "Your dad was treated and released, but you were a different story. There was no brain function, and you were immediately placed on life support. Your dad reached out to me that afternoon, as I'd..." Irene trailed off for a moment. "I'd experienced something similar recently."

I must have looked confused because she sighed and shrugged her shoulders. Her look mirrored dad's at that moment – sad, but resolute.

"There was a convenience store robbery about a year ago. Lillian was inside, paying for gas. She was shot in the head, point-blank. She never even knew it was happening. They kept her on life support for a few days before shutting it down and harvest-" Irene drew in a ragged breath. Apparently, there *was* a limit to a parent's strength. "Harvesting her organs. She was a donor, and her father and I..."

"I'm so sorry," I said. I hadn't known Lillian well, but I remembered a sweet little girl with badly trimmed bangs, who grinned over a PB&J and looked at me like a god when I protected my 8-bit city from space-lasers in *Missile Command*.

Irene just nodded. She needed a moment to consider her next words, and I'd been rude and pushy enough for one day.

"When your father called me, he was ready to discuss what I'd already been through. He was prepared to honor your request. It was me who talked him out of it, Packard. I knew what he was going through, and I couldn't let one of my oldest, dearest friends lose his son without a fight. I wanted to give him, and you, what Lillian and her father and I never got. Hope."

I wanted to argue with her, accuse her of hypocrisy and interfering in other people's personal matters, but I couldn't. Even my jerkiness has its limits.

"Which brings me to where you are right now." Irene motioned around the room like the tour guide at Laboratory 311. "I convinced your father to transfer you to my private medical research facility, Arete Nanophysiology. You're in Cupertino, about three and a half miles from the Winchester Mystery House."

I was still a bit fuzzy around the brain, but nanophysiology sounded like a word I could glean some meaning from. "Nanophysiology? What exactly is that," I asked, unsure I wanted an answer.

"First, I should start with the word Arete. It's an ancient Greek term that means the full realization of potential or inherent function. In Homeric literature, it referred to all the abilities and potentials available to humans. My goal here is to aid in the advancement of human potential itself, to give science the nudge it's been needing for a while now." Irene took a drink of water before continuing. "Nanophysiology, for our purposes – at the core of neural circuit function – is synaptic communication. NCF plasticity allows the nervous system to adapt to changes in its environment. Understanding this, my team and I used a school of Nanops to facilitate synaptic reorganization using your memories stored in your dad's quantum database."

I raised a hand, stopping Irene. "You speak doctor even better than dad. Can you repeat that in, like, teenage English?"

My ignorance elicited a sideways smile from the otherwise stoic Irene. She nodded and laughed softly through her nose. "Sorry, Packard. I forget myself sometimes. I don't get to talk to many non-science types these days. In layman's terms, we coupled my surgical nanotechnology, which I call Nanops, with all the memories you'd created in-game, and essentially rebooted your brain. The data included all your organic memories from before the games and all your waking experiences between games, so it was a safe bet we could bring you back without any memory-lapses."

"Rebooted?" I was stunned. "I'd ask if that was even possible, but we're here talking, so, wow."

"You were a unique case, Packard," Irene said. "How many people do you think actually have a complete backup of their brain lying around? The game consoles Individual Gaming sells have to adhere to super-strict international privacy laws. The consoles scrub several terabytes of identity-specific information from the quantum database uplink after each session. Not to mention, we didn't have time to run human trials or get FDA approval for your procedure."

"So, what you did was illegal," I asked.

Irene responded with a series of long, slow nods. She'd clearly given that fact some thought.

"Yup," she replied finally. "And talking to you right now makes all the risks worth it."

I looked at my dad. He was in the room physically, but his mind was somewhere else. "Dad?" After how I just treated him, I wasn't sure what to say. Screw that. I knew *exactly* what to say. "Dad. I'm sorry."

He looked up at me. His eyes were red, and the surrounding flesh was puffy and raw. He'd been crying for a lot longer than the short time I'd been conscious. He sighed shakily. "I wouldn't have done it if I didn't think you'd have a better quality of life, son. I've done a lot of selfish things in my life, but this was as much for you as it was for me. When Irene approached me with her offer, all I could think was, *my son can finally have the life he deserves.*"

"You don't have a monopoly on selfishness, dad," I said softly. "Thank you for being you, and for not giving up on me."

Dad stepped forward and placed a thin hand on my shoulder. "I love you, Packard. I know I don't always make the right choices, but I do try to put you first whenever I can. I hope you know that."

He wasn't lying. After mom died, he could have gone down the path so many others do when they suffer traumatic loss. Dad could have thrown himself into drugs or alcohol, or the true drug of choice for so many academics, *his work*. He was horribly depressed, yes, but he never allowed his emotional state to affect my world. In fact, when the shit hit the fan, instead of pushing me away, he held me closer. He created a way for me to be involved in his work. When my health deteriorated, he dug his stubborn old heels in even further and created an actual job for me.

"I know, dad." I put my hand over his. "I love you too."

~

Just so you know, I'm not a complete asshat. After dad and I placed a band-aid over our little disagreement, I thanked Irene for clearing the air between us and helping me make sense of what was going on.

Upon finding out why I was alive, I had many questions for the adults in the room.

"I think I understand how you rebooted my brain. You used the backups of my gaming experiences, which, if I understand correctly, contained all my external memories, which you didn't have to scrub because I'm not on the network, right?"

My dad and Irene both nodded. Dad took the floor to answer. "That's a solid understanding, son. The only memories you won't have would be anything following your last gaming session, which was the day before our accident."

"I won't remember what we had for dinner that night, the episode of *Star Trek: Voyager* we probably watched together, or getting into that accident," I joked.

Dad smiled. It was nice to see. "Yeah, that's really it."

"Heck, I don't remember most dinners, so unless something amazing happened in the Delta Quadrant that I should know about, I'm pretty well back to normal then?"

Irene spoke up. "You were mentioning the lack of distinction between organic memories, and residual game data, correct?"

I nodded. "Yeah. Normally it's like the difference between one faucet running hot water and another running cold. They're both water, but it's easy to tell the difference because of the temperature. Now it's like all my memories are running through a single faucet set at warm."

Irene and my father exchanged a brief glance – nothing sinister or unnerving, just two colleagues sharing a contemplative moment. My dad raised an eyebrow, mimicking everyone's favorite Vulcan, tilted his head, and said, "Fascinating."

I couldn't help but laugh at that. Dad was a cornball, and it was good to see him lighten up a bit.

Dad pointed at one of several monitors on the wall. Data streams that reminded me of the code from *The Matrix* scrolled by at impressive speeds. "That's your brain, broken down into binary code," he said. "Or perhaps more accurately, your memories. Just like I used to say in my promo ads, your memories, emotions, fears – everything that makes you who you are, right down to ticks, twitches, and nasty habits."

"Any chance you filtered out nail-biting," I asked.

It was dad's turn to laugh. "Sorry kiddo. As you pointed out, what we were able to give you was a mixed bag at best. We had no way of filtering out specifics without risking losing critical data. It'll take some time, but your brain will eventually sort out what's important and relegate the rest to the darkest recesses of your hippocampus, like arachnodactyls in a cave."

"Okay, *that's* not creepy at all!" Irene nudged dad.

"It's okay," I said. "It wouldn't be dad if there wasn't an occasional bit of creep-factor. It's what makes his games so great."

"Gee, thanks kiddo." Dad grinned, blushing a bit.

"Say, Irene, what was it you were saying about those nano-thingies? You said they helped with the system reboot, but are they also the reason I can feel my legs?" I still wasn't used to the sensations below the waist. Hey, keep your mind out of the gutter! I mean my legs.

Irene's back straightened, and her chin raised a bit as she spoke. I recognized that shift in posture immediately. It was pride. Dad did it whenever he told someone about his games and their unique platform. Considering what she and dad had accomplished with me, they both had the right to be proud. "I call them Nanops, as I designed them to perform complex medical procedures at the atomic level. They started with your brain, reverting your compromised brain cells to an embryonic state to facilitate repair, and fixed the damaged neurons one by one. After that, in the spirit of human potential, they began working on the rest of you. Repairing what was, well, broken, and upgrading the rest."

"Upgrading?" I wasn't sure I was okay with that word. "Like a cyborg or something?"

Irene smiled. "No, nothing like that at all." She paused for a moment, thinking. "More like a booster shot for everything. You've gone from immunocompromised to super immunity. You'll be physically better, mentally sharper, and more

durable. Packard, you represent the next potential step in human

evolution."

10
Expansion Packs

It occurred to me during Irene's extended explanation that the word 'nanops' sounded familiar. It took a few minutes to remember why. "*Tournament of Warlords*," I blurted out.

Irene, whose sciencing made Bill Nye sound like a preschool teacher, stopped and frowned. "Excuse me," she replied.

"*Tournament of Warlords*! Nanops are in the game! Right?"

Dad cleared his throat. "Um, yeah. I might have given them a nod in the game."

Irene arched an eyebrow.

"I liked the name." Dad shrugged. "I did put Arete as the owner of the Nanop trademark, though."

"We can talk about that later," Irene said flatly. She returned her gaze to me. "So, you have a working understanding of what they can do then, yes?"

"If they can heal cuts, bruises, and breaks, and create plasma shields between my arms, then, yeah. If dad took liberties with what they can do, then probably not."

Irene smiled and shook her head at my dad. "Sorry, Packard, but they can't do anything of the sort. Well, the latter anyway. As for healing they can do some amazing things. You're feeling your legs because of them, right?"

I nodded. "Will I be able to walk," I asked.

"Probably," Irene answered cautiously. "If so, perhaps more than just that. Run, jump, dance, skip-"

"Snowboard," I interrupted. "I've always wanted to do that!"

"Let's not get ahead of ourselves." Irene raised her hands slightly, suggesting I pump the brakes on snowboarding for a moment. "Maybe all of the above. And maybe none of it." She wagged an index finger like she was scolding me. "But I'll be honest, I am cautiously optimistic."

~

Once I got past the fact that I was literally being kept alive by machines – exactly the opposite of what I requested – I was pretty excited about the prospects that lay ahead. I was, as Irene put it, 'cautiously optimistic'. Though maybe not quite as cautious as Irene. I never expected to walk again, let alone run or jump. My mind was reeling with ideas. Where I'd go, what I'd do, who I'd do it with. The first two were easy. I wanted to go hiking in the mountains, swim in the ocean, hang-glide over the Grand Canyon, and Disneyland! Man, I wanted to go there. I wanted to ride the Matterhorn and take a selfie with Goofy. I wanted to see Alcatraz

Island, and maybe go dancing at a club. And I wanted to go snowboarding.

As for who I'd do any of those things with? Other than the snowboarding or hang-gliding, I supposed it would be my dad. Oh, and the dancing. Absolutely no dancing. I think dad learned how to dance watching Bruce Springsteen videos on MTV.

It suddenly occurred to me that I'd spent so much time in the gaming world since my health deteriorated, I really didn't have any friends. I never bothered with relationships because I didn't expect to live past twenty-five. I found myself thinking about Becky, Brad, Cool, Dirk, and even crotchety old Clem. They'd been my closest friends for the better part of a decade. Jeez, Santa Claus and a magical dinosaur were more real to me than people I knew as a kid.

Was I that out of touch with the world? Yeah, I guess I was. I suppose it was time to make some new friends.

"How long do I have to stay here," I asked, not really caring which of them answered me. Before either one could open their mouth, I added, "I know you have to run tests and do some poking and prodding. Hopefully not too much of either. And I'm sure there will be physical therapy, and lots of jello and pudding, and..." They stared at me as I babbled. "I'm not letting you answer, am I?"

Dad smirked. "What do you say, Irene? Should we consult with Dr. Packard first?"

Irene shrugged. "It seems like he has all the answers, Hal."

I rolled my eyes, which made me think of Hex, the undisputed queen of eyerolls. "Come on guys, cut me some slack, here. I'm excited! And still a bit nauseous, but mostly excited!"

Dad patted my shoulder. "Irene's the authority on this one," he said. "I'm going to defer to her better judgement."

"Whelp, you're right about the poking and prodding, kiddo," she said grimly. My eyes must have widened to anime-size because she laughed at my expression. "I'm kidding," she said between laughs. "It could be anywhere from a few days to a few weeks." She looked at dad, shrugging like adults do when they have to admit they don't have all the answers. "It really depends on what changes we see and how your body adapts to them. Just so you know, we're most likely looking at the longer end of the estimate. Whatever the results are, good, bad, or neutral, we still want to understand why." Irene looked out the window as she continued. "Whatever happens, kiddo, your dad and I will be here with you to figure things out. Okay?"

"Okay," I replied quietly. "A few weeks, huh?"

"It'll go by like nothing," dad assured me. "Anything you want me to bring from home to make your stay feel less hospital-like?"

"Can I jack into the games," I asked.

Irene put up a hand. "I'm vetoing that request. We don't know how the additional input could affect your brain's ability to process or filter real memories. We need to keep stimulus organic."

Dad looked pensive for a moment. "What about photo albums? Home movies? Things like that?"

Irene nodded. "Those are wonderful ideas. We're in uncharted territory here, and I'd like to keep Packard's brain focused on real memories. We'll monitor his brain function the whole time, of course, to see how certain stimulus affects activity in the hippocampus."

"Well, I know what I'll be doing for the next few weeks," I groaned. "Taking a leisurely stroll down Memory Lane."

11

Memory Lane

As it turned out, Memory Lane is much more pleasant in theory than reality. I'm fairly certain there's a crossroads where Memory Lane and Nightmare Alley meet. There's a used car salesman of a demon waiting there with a contract full of fine-print offering whatever your heart desires. Just sign on the dotted line, pal, and the world is your oyster. Only he never bothered to mention his oysters had botulism.

The dream world was, as dad described my memory dump, a mixed bag. My memories mostly returned when I was asleep, pummeling my subconscious with some incredible, often disturbing visions. Don't get me wrong, I appreciated what dad and Irene did for me, and I knew it would all be fine in the long run. For the time being, though, my psyche was like one of those huge sandwiches Shaggy and Scooby-Doo chowed down on. Instead of lunch meat, lettuce, tomatoes, and cheese, it was layered with panic attacks, nightmares, daydreams, night sweats, and nausea.

To his credit, dad was doing everything he could to stimulate old memories. From photo albums and home movies, to songs I liked and smells I'd always been partial to. In less than a week, my hospital room turned into a shrine dedicated to, well, me. I was surrounded by all things Packard Campbell. A box of old trading cards and action figures sat on a dresser. I'd taken out my Superman, Last Action Hero, and Plastic Man figures and put them on my nightstand. Next to the box of figures was an old record player and a stack of classic albums I'd grown up listening to with mom and dad. The records were theirs, but the music was just as much a part of my soul. Journey, Van Halen, Night Ranger, Joe Satriani, and Sammy Hagar topped the daily playlist, but discounting Jeffster, Phil Collins, Pink Floyd, Boz Scaggs, and so many more foundational artists would have been a mistake. I'm not afraid to admit I cried the day Eddie Van Halen died. Dad did too. He was a hero to both of us, and his music took me back to times long gone.

Poor Irene had to listen to the song "Ice Cream Man" while dad and I sang and giggled more times than she'd ever hoped to hear it, but she was a good sport. She and her husband, George, weren't much for rock. According to her, they normally played classical tunes and occasionally Neil Diamond. But hey, "Sweet Caroline" will always be a classic, right? I promised to introduce her to Panic! At the Disco if dad could find them on vinyl. I'd have pulled them up online, but Irene said the internet would be a potentially bad source of input.

Dad brought me comic books, some of my favorite tee shirts – I have a thing for quirky tee shirts – and my Oakland Raiders sweatpants. Sorry, Vegas, but they'll always be an Oakland team to me. He even brought my favorite coffee mug, a big blue mug with black spots and the word 'HERO' across the front. It was actually a gift for dad from my mom, but he knew how much I liked it, so it became mine by default. The final touch was a stuffed

toy badger I'd had since I was a baby, cleverly named

Badgie. Badgie was old and threadbare, barely held together by

badly done stitch jobs, but she had been my constant companion

as a child. It was fitting for her to be there with me. If anything

could help old memories resurface and take a stronger foothold,

dad packed it into the old Subaru and brought it to me. I was

beginning to wonder if anything of mine, or anything I even

remotely liked, was still at our house.

~

One morning, dad brought in an enormous box and

deposited it at the foot of my bed. He pulled up a chair and

removed an assortment of things that made me wonder if he'd

finally snapped.

He began placing the contents of the box on my nightstand

next to my action figures: a potted plant from our kitchen window,

an old bottle of mom's favorite perfume, a baggie of sand, a small box of computer parts, and a pair of my dirty socks. On the other nightstand he placed a bag of buttered movie popcorn from the Century theaters, a box of salt water taffy from the Santa Cruz Boardwalk, a to-go container of Chinese food, and a ziplock bag full of crispy bacon. As he removed the larger box from the foot of the bed, something inside clinked against the edge. He reached inside and, smiling, produced a set of car keys attached to one of those tacky Christmas tree air fresheners. He set the keys on the nightstand close to the actions figures but was careful to not let them touch the socks.

Irene grinned as I looked back and forth between the nightstands and shrugged. "That's smart," she said. "Smells are another critical link to synaptic retrieval. Your dad is taking his job as the chief archaeologist to your memories very seriously."

"Chief archaeologist to his memories, eh?" Dad smirked. "Sounds like you've been hanging around with Packard and me a bit too much."

Irene nodded, still grinning. "Yeah, I've thrown George off with some of my more colorful phraseology lately, but he stands behind what we're doing, 100%. He said he likes this side of me. It's mysterious and dangerous." Her smile briefly became something I hadn't seen before, or sadly, since. *Genuine.* "He said to tell you both hello, by the way."

"I've never met George," I said.

"He'd like you," Irene replied. "But he's a nano-holography and hard-light optics engineer, so you'd probably find him a bit stiff and boring."

"Hey, any fan of 'Sweet Caroline' is a friend of mine." I winked.

Dad motioned at the two nightstands. "What do you think, kiddo? Wanna start sniffing up some memories?"

I wrinkled my nose. "You brought dirty socks, dad? Seriously?"

Dad shrugged. "It was the only thing I could find that summed up the smell of your bedroom so completely."

Irene covered her mouth, as dad's joke caused her to laugh out loud. "Wow, Packard," she said. "Not even a warning shot first."

"I'll remember that. War is a dirty thing," I replied slyly, reaching for the socks. One whiff of their Pepe Le Pew-like odor and I had to hold them away from my face. It was all I could do to resist throwing them back at dad.

"Arm's length isn't enough, son. Believe me, I tried."

He was right, of course. Both about the smell having a better reach than my arm, and the fact that they immediately made me think of my bedroom. "I hate that you were right about these," I muttered, eliciting another laugh from Irene.

By that time, the memories were coming fast and furious. I must have a strong olfactory recall because everything dad brought pulled another memory to the forefront.

Incredibly, the potted marigolds took me right to our kitchen, and then to our yard, where dad gathered the seeds. They'd been mom's favorite flower. Every spring, she'd plant the seeds from the previous year's blossoms. Memories of my mom, my dad, BBQs in the summer, and smoothies in the kitchen fought for pole-position in my mind. A dog that wasn't ours but spent a month with us while a neighbor was out of the country popped into my mind. A moment later, the dog's smell after it had run around in the rain and then slept on my bed assaulted me. I was remembering smells that weren't even present!

The baggie of sand brought immediate memories of an incredible weekend spent with my parents in Santa Cruz. When dad handed me the box of salt water taffy, the smell and taste of the individually wrapped delights sealed the deal. I was instantly transported to an indoor arcade, where we played air hockey, pinball, *BurgerTime*, and *Centipede*. As with the flowers, more tastes and smells began to flood my memories. I could suddenly taste corn dogs, giant pretzels, and fresh-squeezed lemonade, and the scent of the salt sea-air became intoxicating.

Mom's perfume was arguably the most difficult thing to smell. We've already established that I'm a sentimental old, uh, young fool. I'm not ashamed to say I got choked up. Memories of mom reading to me, hugging me, singing "Don't Stop Believin'", and bandaging my knee when I fell off the neighbor's skateboard swept past my soul like goose down swirling around me in a light wind. They all wanted my attention at once, but were gentle in their insistence to be noticed.

I might have rushed past the perfume a bit abruptly, as it was pretty uncomfortable having dad and Irene see all my emotional responses to the smells. I put the half-full bottle – yep, I'm a 'glass half-full' guy – into the top drawer of my nightstand. Had I known sooner that I could just travel back in my mind so easily, I would have tried aromatherapy years ago.

The collection of computer parts was a bit of a puzzler, but the second I put the box under my nose, my consciousness flashed back to times spent in dad's various workshops and computer labs. Visions of flip-down magnifying glasses, tiny screwdrivers, and soldering irons burned their way to the surface, accompanied by the unique smells of melted soldering wire, slices of Pepperizza Pizza, and spilled Mountain Dew. The smooth stylings of ZZ Top began to thump at the back of my brain, reminding me of dad lumbering around his workshop like an uncoordinated blacksmith. I smiled at dad. Even though he didn't have a clue what I was remembering, he smiled back. He couldn't hide how happy he was if he tried. Suddenly, I felt guilty again for treating him the way I had when I woke up from my brush with eternal slumber. "Thank you, dad," I whispered.

Dad nodded knowingly as he handed me the bag of popcorn. As one might have expected, it started a stream of film clips running in my head that was something like a disjointed string of movie trailers. The experience didn't cause any new memories to surface, but instead helped my brain to better sort the real memories from the game-based recollections. In my state, it was still far too easy to mistake any memories for real ones.

The Chinese food container was full of orange chicken from Sue Lieu's, a Chinese/Vietnamese fusion restaurant near our house in Noe Valley. The smell was amazing. While it didn't do much to fill in any blanks in my memories, it did fill my stomach very nicely.

The last thing was the ziplocked bag of bacon. Amazingly, there was nothing. Zip, zilch, nada. Dad was a bit surprised, but honestly, what can I say? Bacon creates its own memories every time you smell it. It's like an aphrodisiac. It makes you think about wanting something now, not something you wanted last time you had it. That said, let's never talk about aphrodisiacs ever again, please. Okay? Thank you.

As I was munching on bacon, and Irene, who I later learned was a vegetarian, was doing her best to avoid the smell, dad held out the air freshener. "I think you missed something, kiddo," he said.

"I could have used that when you gave me the socks," I lamented. "Now it's just killing the bacon's groove."

Dad laughed. "Sorry, bud. Maybe it was bad timing, but does it make you think of anything?"

I sniffed it, trying to be a good sport. "Your car? Nothing else. Sorry."

"How's about the keys," he asked.

I could tell he was up to something, but most of the time, calling dad cryptic was like calling the Pope Catholic. "The keys?" I got a closer look at the logo when I went to smell the keys. *Pontiac.* "Are these the keys to the GTO, dad?"

Dad was a solidly practical guy. He drove a green, 2014 Subaru Forrester, wore pressed polo shirts, khaki cargo pants, and slip on loafers with long socks. When it got cold, dad would break out one of his dozen or so Mr. Rogers style cardigans, or one of his indGame windbreakers. He had a metric-butt-ton of money from his company, but we lived a modest, middle-class life. Our home belonged to grandma and grandpa Campbell before they passed on, and our furniture, well, mom would have no trouble settling back in if she magically returned from the afterlife. Many people called dad cheap, or boring, but I gave him a pass and called him practical. I honestly never wanted for anything, but for such a techie guy, dad was always most comfortable living in the past. Such a complex mind living such a simple life. Maybe his work life was so full of high-tech, he just preferred his personal life to be low-tech? Or he preferred to surround himself with the simpler, happier times. I never considered any of that before.

Dad nodded.

The car in question was a black, 1965 Pontiac GTO Convertible. Dad bought it in the '80s, restored it, and promptly forgot about it in the garage. I never paid much attention to it because it seemed to be a sore spot for dad. I think he'd always planned to take a long road trip in it with mom. With mom gone and me sick, it became a sad reminder of the things that never happened, and never would.

"I've been tinkering with her," dad said. "I had a friend replace the hoses, belts, and gaskets. She's running again."

"Congratulations," I said, still confused.

"She's yours, son." Dad beamed. "I talked to Irene, and she agreed that while we're working on restoring your old memories, it would be okay to start making some new ones. I never thought I'd get to ask you this, but how would you like your old

man to teach you how to drive?"

12

Crawlspace

Life aboard a space station isn't all Ferengis and giggles. In fact, most space stations aren't anything like the ones on television. Seriously, in all my years as a custodial engineer with the G.O.P.L.C., I have yet to find a spaceport with a bar on board. There are convenience shops of course, but it took all of 5 minutes serving libations to some of the 792 known alien species in a room smaller than a cargo bay, for the Galactic Organization of Peace, Love, and Conformity to realize it was a recipe for disaster. Suffice to say, they made that decision long before my time.

Cheers was great for Bostonians, but Falectors, Sodors, Sabas, Kipums, Rottoxors, and Humans, just don't mix as well as the alcohol does. Truth be told, it's usually humans who start the problems. But hey, why change just because we're in space, right? Humans have a nasty reputation everywhere we go. We're known as the cockroaches of the Milky Way galaxy for a reason, I'd wager. I've even heard some of the more evolved races of intergalactic cockroach take offense to the likening.

My job title is just a fancy term for custodian. I'm a space janitor. I live behind the scenes, kind of like the unseen people who work in the tunnels and behind the walls at Disney World Mars. Life on Dorado IX-XXII is vastly different for each of the individual classes of workers on board. The Chief-Custodian, who isn't actually a custodian, but more of an Overseer, lives in the lap of luxury. She receives the best of everything that passes through her office as payment for her duties. She gets the pick of the food, drink, textiles, tech, you name it. She doesn't get a paycheck, not the way you'd think of it. Nobody on board does. Instead, she's compensated in decadence, a valuable currency when you live on the edge of a newly inducted galaxy group with unquantified resources. She has a stateroom that would make a Grizigian

Warlord jealous, and a wardrobe that would, ummmm, make the same Warlord laugh.

She's flamboyant, but she gets the job done.

As you might have guessed, my compensation is eating, breathing, and hydration. I have a bedroll, clothes, and a set of tools I protect with my life. I sleep wherever I was working when I got tired, and I eat at the slop dispenser. The official name for the slop is Synzymes – synthetic enzymes. I really don't want to know what's in it, but it looks and tastes like slop, so that's what the other grunts and I call it. Fresh water is a luxury we have here on Dorado. There's a cluster of comets that circle through our sector regularly. Our science team siphons off the gasses, filtering out surprising amounts of water vapor.

The maintenance crew and I do our 'business' in small, recessed areas in the floor. The receptacles get flushed hourly with gray water, and our refuse washes into the central incinerator. The worst part of my job, aside from the lack of any privacy during bathroom breaks, is the tightness of the area we work in. Be forewarned, this is not a good career choice for anyone with even the remotest claustrophobic tendencies. Known only as crawlspaces, our home is a 1-meter by 1-meter tunnel system and massive, but short, open areas between the station floors. If you've ever seen an office building under construction, with all the support columns in place, but no furniture or anything populating it, or been under a house, that's what the areas between levels look like. Only 1 meter tall; for anyone who doesn't do the metric thing, it's a little over 3 feet. So, yeah, we actually crawl everywhere we go.

The only place we can get vertical is in the riser shafts that allow us to move between the 42 levels that make up the massive station. We rarely do that because each level has its own fully functioning crew. To put things into perspective size-wise, the station is roughly a mile in diameter, only stacked 42 times, like a terrifying quarter of a mile tall space Jenga tower. It has to be big, though, when you consider it's the primary spaceport for an entire galactic cluster.

There are roughly 100 of me on each floor. Oh, yeah, if I hadn't mentioned it already, I'm a clone. At least, I think I'm a clone. The odds of me being the original are pretty low, but I suppose it's possible, since we're the first generation of clones to man all the G.O.P.L.C's 68 stations. This is my 16th station, and it's my favorite so far. Just kidding. They're all pretty much the same, barless and boring.

Oh, crap, I was talking about being a clone, wasn't I? Yep, we all have the same memories and skills at birth, but we develop our own personalities over time. Some of us like being alone, while others seek companionship. Some like to sing, while others like it quiet. And some of us even like music. I put in a requisition for a ukulele, so I can play during my downtime. I mean, there's one of me that has a harmonica. How's that fair? Hmm, maybe he's the original, and they're playing favorites.

Oh well. Maybe I'll just ask for a nice juice-harp instead. Or a pan flute. Or a freakin' spoon and washboard. I just want some music. Is that so wrong?

My name's John, by the way. We're all Johns. I'm John Cocktolstoy. I would have preferred Smith or Jones, but with almost 300,000 of us in service, they had to get creative with some of our last names. My surname is Scotch-Romanian, or at least that's what Mr. Fletcher and Dr. Rosenrosen told me.

My closest, um, me, that I work with, is John Lev. He's the one with the harmonica. In our quadrant, floor 12, sector 7, there's me, John, John, John, John, and John. I suppose last names would probably help. There's me, Lev, Nugent, Babar, Stravinsky, and Corleone. We occasionally team up with Poppins and Nostradamus, but only when we're flushing out the air exchange system. Most of what we do is done alone or in pairs.

I'm one of the Johns who likes solitude. I have a routine that allows me to get most of my work done with minimal contact, which is how I got into the predicament I was in when we started this conversation.

Remember the riser shafts I mentioned earlier? I was in one when the shit hit the fan. At that point, I wasn't going anywhere. I was holding onto the ladder and trying to stay as quiet as humanly possible. Any movement would echo up and down the shafts and out into the crawlspaces, attracting some very unwanted attention.

I was on the ladder, allowing my back to get a long overdue stretch, when the screams began. Did I mention I was hanging upside down by my knees?

~

You may be thinking, *that's a crappy position to be in during a crisis.* You'd be right. I only wanted to hang for a minute or so. It does wonderful things for my back, considering I crawl around the tunnels like the Shire's largest hobbit most of the time. But I'd been hanging upside down like a Brarrian blood-bat in an uakitite mine for more than 20 minutes at that point. My eyes felt like they were ready to pop out of my skull just to let everything else inside me drain out.

Whatever the hell was out there was hunting the other Johns. Considering how quiet things suddenly sounded, I was afraid I was the only one left.

When the screams began, other awful noises followed. Noises that would've made your skin crawl, and the blood run cold in your veins. Inhuman shrieks and undulating hoots accompanied eerie dragging and scraping, and a high-pitched whine I could feel in my bones.

When the screaming stopped, so did most of the other noises. All I could hear was something being dragged across the metallic floor, and that awful, echoing hoot. Think of what it looks like when you hold two mirrors at an angle and get that infinite mirror effect, then imagine that visual as a sound. Yeah, that's what the hoot sounds like. It diminishes but it never quite sounds like it's ever really gone. It's terrifying.

I really had to pee, but being upside down made that concept almost as horrifying as whatever was out there hunting us.

As I hung, and my head and bladder competed for the right to complain, I listened to the dragging sounds. I realized they were coming from multiple directions. Worse yet, some of them were getting closer.

I closed my eyes and focused on the awful, mind-numbing sounds. We clones had some of our senses and natural abilities enhanced to allow us to not only survive but thrive in less than perfect conditions. I wasn't exactly superhuman, that cost a lot of money. Only celebrities, corporate CEOs, career criminals, and politicians —maybe those last two were redundant – were wealthy enough for those kinds of enhancements.

I had a few, um, upgrades. Abilities added to the original at the genetic level and passed down to all the clones cheaply. In addition to markers for enhanced strength and endurance, I have a greater resistance to otherwise 'disagreeable' temperatures, and the ability to function on lower levels of oxygen. I can also see extremely well in the dark, and of course, the whole reason I went off on this tangent, I have exceptional hearing.

The odd chorus of dragging sounds was the most prominent and clearly the closest. I could also make out the occasional groan, which I figured was one or more of my fellow Johns. To make things worse, somewhere in the distance I could hear something chewing on something else, the victim also assumed to be one of my poor legion of Johns.

I tilted my head slightly, both to loosen a kink in my neck, and to get a better grasp on how close the sounds were.

And that's when I saw the caterpillars.

~

Caterpillars? You're probably thinking, *how scary could a caterpillar be?* Well, normally I'd say they're one of the cutest damn things in nature, especially the fuzzy little guys. But these things were anything but cute. Their bodies were about 8 inches long and looked like caterpillars, but that was where the similarities ended. These guys had legs that looked like 3 inch long possum tails, pink scaly skin, gross wiry hair and all. They didn't appear to have any eyes, but at the front of what I assumed was their head were several circles of teeth. Each of the circular sets of teeth was set behind another, like a baby lamprey. The smallest, center-most set, clicked harmlessly around a needle-sharp tongue. I really hoped that was the head. It would be a horrifying butt.

Oh, and if the description doesn't mess with your day, then consider this. When I noticed the little bastards there were more than a dozen of them, just chilling, about 10 inches from my face.

Yeah. There I was, staring at a bunch of tiny nightmares, when I heard the screech beneath me.

I looked down just in time to see one of the Johns from another floor, either Harley or Lemonjello, I think, coming up the ladder underneath me. He looked like he was in a lot of pain, and I almost reached out for him. Then I saw the movement on his back. As he arched, trying to free himself of whatever was on him, I could see a swarm of the carnipillars – yeah, I named them – on his back. They were crawling around, just out of his reach, repeatedly stinging him with their tongues… or maybe they were their butts after all. Yikes!

Remaining still had been the right thing to do. The moment John opened his mouth to scream, the carnipillars I'd unwittingly been sharing space with dropped onto his face and shoulders. They stung him repeatedly. One of them even climbed into his mouth, causing him to bat at it with his free hand. Eventually, the pain must have overwhelmed him. John let go of the rung he was holding and dropped. It was 12 stories down to the bottom of the

riser, and I heard every awful second of John's descent. He was

probably dead before he hit the bottom. Even with our enhanced

durability, none of us could survive a 12-story drop.

I looked up again, only to find the wall above me covered

with the little Lovecraftian devil worms. I had no idea what they

were, or where they came from, but after seeing what they did to

John, I wasn't going to stick around to ask them!

Taking hold of the rung closest to the 12th level crawlspace,

I pulled my knees away from their perch and swung myself back

into my 3-foot-tall workspace. The carnipillars dropped

immediately, but they, like John, continued down the riser

shaft. Considering their size, the impact probably didn't kill

them. I needed to get away from the riser, fast!

I rolled over and discovered two terrifying things. My legs

were completely numb from hanging upside down for more than

20 minutes, and the other Johns weren't dead. At first, I was

relieved to make the second discovery, but that elation was short-lived. The moment they saw me, they all screeched in unison and crawled after me like a pack of rabid gophers.

The horrifying carnipillars covered every John. They weren't stinging anymore, so I assumed they'd achieved whatever their goal had been with my fellow clones. The worms raised their heads/butts like cobras preparing to strike and rode my fellow workers into battle like an unholy cavalry.

Whatever they'd done to my poor, unfortunate coworkers, they wanted to do to me next.

~

As the Johns and their overzealous cargo bore down on me, I tried to kickstart my legs into helping me out of their way. See what I did there? Kick? Kickstart? Legs? No? Aww, forget about it.

Anyway, my bladder finally decided it'd had enough, and as I frantically dragged myself away from my pursuers, I left an impressive puddle of urine in my wake. There was no place for it to go, so it just spread out in all directions.

As I scrambled forward like a walrus on ice, the five Johns learned why the bodily function disposal receptacles existed. The moment they hit the urine, they slipped and slid in every direction except the way they wanted to go. My bladder scored us a head start!

Unfortunately, my victory was short-lived. Those darned carnipillars seemed to be coming from everywhere, and if you've given much thought to the layout of my little world, then you understand I have nowhere to effing go!

I scuttled into one of the tunnels. On the surface, that might've seemed like the worst place to put myself, but from a defensive standpoint, I only had two directions to defend instead of a 360° attack-zone. I made my way to a 90° left turn and backed into the corner, where I could see down both tunnels. The news coming from either direction was not good.

If I was on the security team, the suppression force, or the invasion squad, I might have stood a good chance against the carnipillars and their Zombie-Johns, but dammit, I'm a janitor, not a soldier!

I dug into my tool bag, which was intentionally devoid of any weapons, and found a few things I'd never considered to be particularly dangerous in the past. First was my multi-use krail; a bull-nosed, machete-like blade designed to separate access panels, strip wires, and pry up floor tiles. Next out were my brillin shears, super sharp and extra durable wire and conduit cutters. The last thing to come out of my bag was my gel-based plasma torch. Considering the name, it doesn't require an explanation. The torch was for welding, cutting, freeing frozen conduit, and sometimes heating my slop. Now I was hoping it would save my life!

My torch had been on the fritz for several. I'd requested a replacement for the flow-control valve, which restricted the flame output to keep it safe and manageable. My flame, as it stood, was hardly what one could consider safe. I got an 18-inch jet of heated plasma instead of the station regulated 6 inches. I had good old-fashioned bureaucracy to thank for my increased odds of survival. How could I say I really expected a ukulele when I had to fight for safe equipment? John Lev was definitely the original.

Johns and carnipillars were fast approaching from both sides! My identical counterparts were clearly not in control of their own bodies, and I wasn't looking to find out what was in the driver's seat the hard way. I fumbled in my bag once more and found that I had almost a dozen gel cartridges.

I slammed one into the bottom of my torch and clicked off the safety. As I picked up my krail with my free hand, I pulled the trigger.

~

My faithful torch sparked to life and an 18-inch focused jet of flame belched forth, all but searing the face off the John approaching from my left. The jet also caught a half dozen or so carnipillars. They fell to the floor, sizzling and popping, resembling Cajun Spiced Cheetos.

I twisted to the right and treated another oncoming John to a mouthful of flame, sealing the deal with a blow to the head from my krail. Carnipillars flew from John's dying body, some reduced to writhing black husks. The rest stopped in their tracks, obviously considering whether I was worth the risk. One of the more brazen carnipillars decided to bum-rush me from a potential blind spot, but I reduced it from brazen to brazed with a flick of my torch. The remaining mini monsters drew back to a safe distance. They chose *wisely*. They continued to back away, using the bodies of the other Johns as a shield. Right then I recognized my mistake. If I tried to escape in either direction, I would have to push past one of the dead Johns, and then avoid being stung by the carnipillars behind the John. That would be hard enough, but there were still carnipillars hiding behind the other John, waiting to attack as soon as I let my guard down.

I was racking my brain, trying to come up with an alternative, when the first John, whom I'd thought I'd killed, began to move again. He raised his face slowly and stared at me, his remaining good eye pleading. His mouth fell open in an unheard scream and a carnipillar leg thrust out like a drowning person's hand from a Dinerinan grease-swamp. Only it wasn't exactly like the legs. I mean, it was, only a lot larger. Like 3 feet, instead of 3 inches!

Suddenly, John began to convulse and spasm like an orangutan attempting the limbo. Before I could shield my eyes, his back ripped open from neck to tailbone, freeing more of the possum tail-like legs that pushed out in a horrifying wave!

Then came the wings.

For an odd moment, I was relieved they weren't veined and fleshy like a bat's wings, but smooth and silky like a moth's. Then the gore that had once been John slipped off them, and they spread to fill the 3-foot wide tunnel before me. I realized they could have been made of peanut butter and jelly – I really love PB&J – and they would still be horrifying, maybe even more so.

The thing sloughed off John like a cocoon. In retrospect, that was exactly what he'd been. Its wings shook like a dog coming in from the rain, and I got my first and only good look at the awfulness that had grown so quickly inside my fellow custodian. Its massive body was still segmented and caterpillar-like, and even in the hazy, green lighting, I could tell it was arterial-red. The pink, scaly, hair-covered legs shifted backwards, becoming a hydra of a tail, each appendage whipping back and forth dangerously, beating rhythmically against each other and the tunnel walls. Six spindly legs, each lined with several rows of black barbed spikes, supported Mo'thulhu. Completing the list of things I never wanted to see was the creature's head. Huge, black, glossy eyes stared into my soul, and I, like a fool, stared back into the emptiness of the abyss. Two feathery antennae unfurled like terrifying snakes uncoiling to strike, and one of them brushed against me. The brush shocked me back into action. As I held my torch out in front of me, preparing to squeeze the trigger, I saw the monster's tongue dart out from beneath its eyes. The needle tongue looked like a crossbow bolt. It flicked forward, hungrily searching for whatever the antennae had encountered.

I squeezed the trigger on the torch. Nothing happened.

I raised my krail and gave the best swing I could manage in such tight quarters. I lopped off the front of the monster's face, including its spike of a tongue, and without thinking, crawled back towards John #2.

Hearing scuttling behind me, I turned just in time to see more carnipillars skirting John's corpse. I held up the torch, and they retreated to the safety of their John-shield. They were quick learners. That didn't really help me, since they would soon learn all about the concept of empty threats.

Nowhere to go, I thought grimly. And then it occurred to me, the one place I might be safe.

I looked for the telltale line of a paper-thin gap between the floor tiles. When I found it, I slid my krail between them, and pried. I said *pried*, not cried. Don't misread me here.

The heavy metal tile popped up and slid aside with relative ease. I was happy to find an entire water system flushing apparatus, which I promptly pulled out, and pushed in the direction of the second John who just started doing the chrysalis boogie. I was not interested in facing another mini kaiju!

Removing the massive apparatus from the floor space left a sizeable opening where I could hide something big, like myself.

As I dropped into the open space, and the carnipillars tentatively ventured forward, I spotted something worth risking my life for. I reached out and swiped it from the floor in front of John #1. It fell from his shirt pocket as he gave birth to Mo'thulhu. A carnipillar scuttled towards my hand, its awful spike waving like a tiny doctor with a syringe of death. I smashed it with my fist before pulling back my arm and forcing the tile back into place, sealing myself inside like an Egyptian Pharaoh on a trip to the afterlife.

I curled up in the cramped space, knowing a small water line ran just inches from my face. With the water line and the ration bars in my bag, I could survive there for several days, if not weeks.

Like I said before, not the job for a claustrophobe.

In the dim glow of the emergency lighting that filtered through the gaps above me, I settled in and listened to my personal symphony of death. The shrieks of approaching Johns and the scratching of hundreds of carnipillars that wanted to lay eggs in me composed the bloodcurdling mock orchestra.

After a few moments of listening to the evil cacophony, I joined the macabre din with my own musical contribution, courtesy of John Lev's harmonica.

Then the pounding started. The second Mo'thulhu had apparently been freed and was trying to get to me.

That was when I finally cried. Yes... *cried.*

13

Hal Campbell

I awoke with a frightened cry, startling dad and Irene. It wasn't the first bad dream I'd woken from since being rezzed. I'd had several. Some of them were related to things that happened in real life, while others were clearly gameplay related. Many of them ended with me dying of dysentery. I swear, I will never play *Oregon Wagon Train* again for as long as I live.

My dad approached the bed, trying his best to look calm, but instead just coming off as haggard and tired.

Dad had been through a lot over the past decade. Between losing mom, and then me getting sick and then dying, well, he'd been through just about all a person could endure and retain their sanity. He earned the right to look haggard. No, to hell with that noise. He'd done nothing to earn the crap hand dealt to him. It had been thrust upon him like a plague, and still, he remained strong. Poker face and all.

I didn't tell him nearly enough. "Thank you, dad," I said as he placed a frail-looking hand on my shoulder.

He looked puzzled. "For what?"

I patted the hand on my shoulder. "For that. And everything else you do."

"I'm your dad," he started.

"And you're a good one," I interrupted.

He smiled. "That means the world to me, son." His voice cracked, and he turned towards Irene, hoping I wouldn't see him wipe a tear from his cheek.

He was an old softie. Mom loved him until her last breath, and he would love her, and me, until his.

~

Dad's birth name was Hal. Just Hal. Like the rogue computer in *2001: A Space Odyssey*. He thinks it's funny when he tells me, "I'm sorry, Dave. I'm afraid I can't do that." The house has seen endless, often one-sided, bouts of laughter over that one. He thinks a lot of the things he says are funny and who am I to disagree? If his jokes make him happy, I don't have to understand them all. I usually just laugh with him.

Anyway, Hal is an Irish name that means 'Chief'. I tried calling dad chief once when I was about thirteen. He clearly didn't like it, and it felt too weird rolling off my tongue. I dropped it after one attempt. It's like kids who call their parents by their first names. I'll never get that.

Our last name came from the surname Mac Cathmhaoil, also Irish. When my great-grandparents immigrated from Europe, they met the fun folks on Ellis Island, who clearly weren't qualified for their jobs, since they didn't understand how to pronounce or spell anyone's last names outside the continental United States. How do you put people like that in charge of greeting immigrants to a new country anyway? Welcome to America, Mister uh, Mac Cat… uh, *Campbell.* Yeah, that'll do. From now on, you're the Campbells.

I like my last name, but it had to be weird for my great-grandparents trying to adjust. They'd already given up everything they'd ever known, and they couldn't even keep their own last name?

Oh sorry, I was telling you about dad, wasn't I? I squirreled again.

My dad was born in the early 70s. He got his first Atari system when he was five or six. Since grandma and grandpa Campbell were fairly well-off, they upgraded him to an Atari 400 a couple years after that. The 400 came with a Basic cartridge that allowed for some, well, basic programming. Dad learned at an early age how to make a few simple animations and program 'conditional' style games, and the rest was history.

The 80s and 90s were an amazing time for dad, each decade coming with unique challenges and rewards. Dad got involved in Virtual Reality in the 80s while he was still a teenager. Yeah, VR was a thing even back then. In fact, the first VR headset, *The Sword of Damocles*, came out in 1968, well before dad's time.

Dad dove deep into Augmented Reality in the early 90s, and by Y2K, he had single-handedly pioneered Neural Reality. His early gaming consoles were, and probably still are, used by the U.S. military and other covert divisions for training purposes. Think of Will Smith's famous line when he sparred with Sean Connery in *The Matrix*. "I know kung fu." Yeah, dad invented that in the real world.

Mom and dad met at a tech convention in Las Vegas in 2001. A year later, on February 21st, they tied the knot. A little more than a year after that, I came along.

~

Mom was amazing. Honestly, the decade she and dad had together before she passed, made him the man he needed to be to raise me on his own. She loved dad dearly, but he had a few minor quirks. Mostly, he was a workaholic. As much as he loved work, he loved mom and me more, which was how he adapted to family life. He didn't change because she told him to, or even because she asked politely. He changed because we were important to him. It's what people do when they discover there's something, or someone, they love more than themselves.

Dad always focused on his company. IndGame is clearly a labor of love, but he also made time for the people he loved. Dad was rational and inventive, which made him a natural-born problem solver. Despite being logical and realistic, dad was also imaginative and loved considering unique possibilities, which was why he was born to own and run Individual Gaming. He brought all the necessary elements to the table. Of course, there are the obvious traits that exist in all great leaders, he was visionary, inspirational, dependable, and creative. Beyond that, dad possessed open-mindedness, a saintly level of patience, and flawless authenticity. Those last three traits, though, mom discovered and cultivated them. Because while he learned them, she had lived them.

Mom was the perfect example of the strength behind the leader, the wind beneath the proverbial wings. Sadly, a piece of dad went with her when she died.

You already know what happened after mom died and I got sick. Dad continued life exactly like she was still looking lovingly over his shoulder, whispering words of encouragement into his ear. What I haven't shared is that for the first time in my young life, I saw my dad put up a facade. Day in and day out, he wore a brave mask meant for me and a few people who worked closely with him at indGame. But each night, after he tucked me safely in my bed, I could hear dad sigh and trudge off to bed alone. He didn't know it, but I could hear him talking to her most nights, like she was right there in the room with him. Other nights he'd just cry.

Dad stayed strong for me when she died and upped the ante when I got sick. Who was there for dad? Certainly not me.

"Hey, dad," I asked, breaking the silence again.

"Yeah, son?" He looked at me through the same concerned lens he'd been viewing me through for the past eight years. He still saw me as fragile, breakable.

"I can't wait to spend time with you, dad," I said.

"We *are* spending time together, pal," he replied, not understanding what I was trying to say.

"I mean when we're away from here." I glanced at Irene. "Sorry, no offense."

"None taken." She smiled.

"I'm looking forward to doing things together, dad. Things we couldn't do before. I want to help out around the house. You know, mow the lawn, clean out the rain-gutters, *paint the house?*" I added extra emphasis to the last task. Our house needed a fresh coat of paint as much as I needed a day out in the fresh air.

Dad looked genuinely taken aback. "I don't know what to say."

"You don't have to say anything now, dad." I winked. "But you can say 'thank you' when we start seeing some progress around the house."

14

Home

The next day was a good one, if not a bit on the weird side. I'll remember it forever, for so many reasons.

It started with dad and Irene announcing that I was finally going home. But if I told you right now how it ended, well, what would be the point of telling you my story?

~

As we packed my room to move all my earthly belongings back to our home in San Francisco, it again occurred to me how much care and thought dad put into my rehabilitation. Dad or not, he and Irene went above and beyond on every possible front, and I would never let them forget how appreciated they were. Heck, I figured I owed a letter of thanks to Irene's husband, George, by that time too.

An Arete Nanophysiology security guard most professional football players would call 'sir' carted several boxes out to dad's car. He looked like if King Kong decided to cosplay Mr. T. His name tag said 'Gunner', but he didn't need firearms to be intimidating.

Dad picked up a box full of comic books, grunting at the weight. Gunner nodded at the three stacked boxes he was already carrying. "Put it up here," he said, sounding every bit as tough as he looked.

Dad shook his head, but Gunner insisted.

Dad hefted the box up and set it atop the stack with a sigh.

Gunner just nodded and strolled to the door like he was carrying a stack of feather pillows.

Dad ran ahead of the guard. I could hear him panting in the hall. "At least let me get the elevator for you!"

I could practically hear Gunner nodding politely. "Why, thank you," he said, a slight chuckle in his voice.

The elevator dinged happily in the hall, and dad returned with a smile. "He had quite a load there, kiddo," he proclaimed. "I couldn't let him do that all on his own."

I nodded. "Does he have the car keys," I asked.

Dad facepalmed himself comically. "Crap." He ran out the door as Irene came in carrying a file folder.

"Everything okay," she asked.

"I think dad's going to challenge Gunner to a pose-off," I said, smirking.

Irene laughed and shook her head. "I'm going to miss you being here, Packard," she said, handing me the folder. "I haven't laughed this much in, well, ever." She shook her head again. "Even George is developing a sense of humor. He said that between you and your dad, the silliness has been rubbing off on me, and he's in 'if you can't beat 'em, join 'em' mode."

"I'll email you more jokes," I told her. "We have to keep George on his toes, otherwise all of our hard work was for nothing." I looked at the folder in my hands. "What's this," I asked, even though I knew I could find out by opening it.

"Open it," Irene instructed.

~

Dad returned to find me flipping through several pages of printed documents. I paused occasionally on the ones that included pictures or diagrams, but even those were well beyond my comprehension.

"Whatcha' got there, kiddo," he asked, still huffing from chasing Gunner.

"Hermione Granger, here, thought I might like a bit of light reading," I replied.

Dad smirked, but the joke was clearly lost on Irene. I closed the folder and turned back to her. "So, since I'm gonna to have to complete multiple degrees in particle physics, nanophysics, and molecular biology before I can read any of this, wanna give me the Cliffs Notes version?"

Irene missed the Hermione Granger joke but smiled at the Cliffs Notes quip. I was either losing my touch, or she was completely out of touch. It had to be the latter.

Irene assumed the 'proud' pose again, chin up and shoulders back. "It's essentially a user's manual for the Nanop technology. I originally dubbed them MOIs, or Mothers of Invention, but that was too clunky, so I stuck with Nanops."

Dad appeared impressed. "I didn't know you were a Frank Zappa fan."

Irene's expression looked like a Vulcan asked to do standup comedy. "I don't know what the former president has to do with nanotechnology, but I'm assuming there's a joke hidden in there?"

Dad put up a hand in mock-surrender. "No jokes," he replied. "Please, continue."

Irene nodded, then smiled. "Sorry, when I get into nano-mode, it's hard to distinguish me from my bots."

"So why do I need this," I asked Irene. "I've got you to answer my questions, right?"

Irene shifted uncomfortably, her smile fading. "Yes, but as we are all painfully aware, accidents happen. If anything happens to me, answers to any questions you have about the technology inside you are in there." She seemed to think for a moment before continuing. "The Nanops, Packard, they're a part of you now. Your dad, me, George, we're not going to be around forever. It's conceivable that, with the bots inside you, your lifespan could be considerably longer than the average person. That information is mostly a safety net, or a blueprint. I'm a just in case girl if you know what I mean?"

Considering dad and Irene resurrected me with experimental technology and a video game backup, it took a lot to surprise me at that point. When Irene mentioned a 'considerably longer' lifespan, though, it floored me. "Can we back up a few words, please, Irene," I asked. "How much is *considerably longer*?"

Irene shrugged. It wasn't one of those dismissive shrugs most adults offer when the question is more than they want to think about, or they're embarrassed to admit they don't have an answer. It was a 'we're in uncharted territory, here, kiddo' shrug.

"We're in uncharted territory, here, Packard," she said.

Damn, I was good.

She maintained the type of eye contact that indicated a serious dose of truth. "I don't have a concrete number, but I can tell you 1000 years ago, in Ancient Greece and Rome, the average life expectancy was 20 to 35. In the 1960s, the average increased to the low 50s. Today, with fewer wars and all the approved medical advances, it's not unreasonable for someone to live into their 80s. You, uh, might live a lot longer than that."

Even dad seemed surprised by the revelation. "Are you sure of this, Irene," he asked.

"I'm not *sure* of anything," she replied. "Like I've been saying since we first agreed to attempt this, we've already stepped off the precipice, Hal. We're standing in open space."

All I could picture at that moment was dad, Irene, and me standing in midair with Wile E. Coyote, with me holding up a little 'Yikes!' sign on a stick.

"What I *can* say," Irene continued, "is that we've been successful thus far. I see zero reason to believe we have anything to worry about."

Dad still looked concerned. I'll admit, the idea of living a lot longer than anyone else I'd ever know or love, was a bit jarring.

Irene patted my shoulder. "Would I be sending you home if I didn't think you'd be fine?" She tilted her head a bit, keeping that intense, motherly eye contact. "You know me better than that by now, yes?" She looked at dad, meeting his eyes as well. "Yes?"

Dad nodded. He and I finally spoke in unison. "Yes."

Irene smiled thinly. "Okay then. I'm sorry that never came up before, guys. There are so many variables we're going to have to explore together as we go. Agreed?"

Again, our response was in stereo. "Agreed."

Gunner popped into the room, dad's car keys dangling from an outstretched hand. The air in the room must have been thick with the potential for drama because he stopped dead in his tracks in the doorway. His eyes narrowed suspiciously as he observed the scene like a true security professional. "So, what'd I miss?"

~

You're probably wondering how I was getting out of that place. Wheelchair? Crutches? Well, if you guessed 'on my own two feet', you'd be right! I suppose I could have told you about this earlier, but it happened so quickly, and with so much less pain or indignity than any of us anticipated, it kinda fell out of my head. One day I was telling Irene I could feel my legs, the next, I walked to the window on my own. After that, there were trips to the bathroom, the fridge, and even the occasional walk down to the elevator. Come on, you've done it too. Pressing all the buttons and sending it to all the floors by itself? It's great fun imagining people seeing an empty elevator open, wondering who was getting out, then wondering why nobody did. No? Man, you're missing out.

Anyway, I hadn't done any running, skipping, dancing, or skiing yet, but those still topped my list of things to do.

Considering I never expected to walk again, it's an easy thing to take for granted. I feel like I did that with a lot of things. People, too. My plan was to never take anything for granted, ever again.

~

Once we left Arete Nanophysiology, the day went too fast.

Dad surprised me with a spur of the moment visit to the world-famous Winchester Mystery House before heading back north. It was a Tuesday, so it wasn't busy.

It was everything I'd ever expected and more. If you're not familiar with it, the landmark was the former home of Sarah Winchester, heiress to the Winchester rifle fortune. A Boston-based psychic told her the spirits of every victim of the Winchester rifles were coming after her. She believed that continuously building her home in odd, unpredictable directions would confuse the ghosts and keep her safe. I guess nobody ever told her ghosts could walk through walls, eh?

Anyway, the home is incredible, beautiful, and yes, very confusing. The bored-looking, slack-jawed tour guide, who was probably around dad's age, told us there were forty staircases, two-thousand doors, forty-seven fireplaces, and upwards of ten-thousand windows. They discovered a hidden attic in 2016, upping the room count to a staggering one hundred and sixty-one. The place was crazy! In a little over an hour, dad and I saw doors that opened to walls, staircases that stopped at the ceiling, and fully functioning windows in floors. The late Mrs. Winchester even went as far as to sleep in a different room every night. Can you guess why? Yup, to confuse those pesky ghosts.

Speaking of ghosts, during the tour I'm sure I saw one, or at least the outline of one, twice. It was a creepy old gunfighter-looking cowboy. I saw him first in the grand ballroom, then again at the end of one of the halls. He flickered in and out of existence like a character in the old A-Ha video, "Take On Me". On both occasions, the entire group was looking in the same direction as me. Nobody else seemed to notice the apparition, so I kept my observations to myself. I didn't want dad to think I was losing touch with reality on my first day outside the facility.

After the mansion tour, we drove a few miles south and visited the house mom and dad owned before moving to San Francisco. It was down the street from an upscale shopping plaza called The Pruneyard. The little town's name was Campbell, of all things. I felt like I should get a Campbell keychain or something, but I quickly learned not all towns indulged in touristy paraphernalia.

The tiny, 3-bedroom house was pale yellow and sported white trim that made it look like it belonged in an old Disney feature, like *Snow White* or *Pinocchio*. Dad and I parked out front for a few minutes, just staring, before a young woman with a baby on her arm peered out the front picture window. She was obviously wondering who the creepers out front were, and was probably considering a call to the cops, so dad sighed and pulled away from the curb.

From the tiny house on Decorah Lane, we drove up the road to one of my favorite childhood memories, the car wash. Yeah, you heard that right, the car wash. Let me tell you, this was not just any car wash. It was a Riverboat! Look, you've never really had your car washed until you've driven it through a replica of an old Riverboat. Seriously. I had to beg dad to do it, but by the time we were there, I could see he needed the memory-therapy as much as I did. Besides, the house had left him all weepy and melancholy. We had more than an hour's drive home, and he needed to be in better spirits for the trip.

Once the car was all shiny and as new looking as dad's trusty steed could get, a solid case of the hungries hit. Naturally, we went to The Red Barn for a Double-Barnbuster and a Coke!

As had been customary before I got sick, dad and I picked a corner booth, and we spoke in between bites. Look, I know it's supposed to be rude, but man it felt good, just sitting there with dad, eating a burger and shooting the breeze. It was the closest thing to normal I'd felt in years. I wanted to savor the time and conversation as much as I wanted to savor every bite of that incredible burger and fries. In truth, even though it was the first burger I'd been able to eat in about five years, the food couldn't hold a candle to the quality time with dad.

As we finished our meal, dad offered me his last few fries, which I gladly accepted. "Good burger, kiddo," he asked.

"It's not Irene's Jello salad, but it'll suffice," I said through a mouthful of fries. Then it occurred to me. "You know what we didn't do?"

"What? Did we not wash our hands first," he asked.

"Um, dang. Dad, we're gross, you know that?" I thought about it for another moment before pushing the last few fries back to the center of the table. "It wasn't that, but thanks for the reminder." I shrugged. "We forgot a strawberry shake."

Dad's eyes grew. "Your mom's favorite."

Then, in unison, we both said, "For dipping her fries."

"Wow," dad said, "I'd almost forgotten."

"We both did," I said before standing up. "I'm going to wash my hands now."

When I returned from the bathroom, dad had a small strawberry shake and a small order of fries on a tray in the middle of the table. He smiled. "Care to share?"

I nodded, not even trying to hide how cool that was. "Only if you wash your hands first."

~

The drive home was nice. Traffic was surprisingly light for a Tuesday afternoon. We only had to slow down twice, once going through the Los Altos Hills, and again around Woodside for some dude who decided peeing on the side of the highway was a clever idea.

By the time we got to the Noe Valley, traffic was characteristically thick. The trip took us just over an hour. In that time, we listened to a few episodes of my favorite podcast, which I hadn't heard in almost five months. The podcast, *Erica's Podcast of Cosmic Horrors and Weirdly Weirdness*, was also one of dad's favorites. As much as we talked during our meal, we were silent during the podcast. Unless you call the occasional slurp from a straw, the catching of our breath, or low whistles, conversation.

The episode was creepy enough, but the old cowboy I'd seen on the tour kept popping back into my head. I'm a bit of a nihilist, so I never really believed in ghosts, but I know I saw something. The podcast was pouring gasoline on the imaginary fire.

The third episode was about to end as we pulled into the driveway. Rather than stop at the climax, we sat in the garage next to the Pontiac, *my* Pontiac, with the A/C running as we listened to the tale of Nyarlathotep and his conquest of a Mayan tribe in early Mesoamerica. Chilling stuff, even giving some of dad's games a run for their money.

"How the hell does she come up with that stuff," dad wondered aloud as he popped the hatchback.

"People probably wonder the same thing about you, dad," I parried.

He smiled, grabbing a box. "Touché."

"Let me help you, dad," I said, reaching for one as well.

Dad practically swatted me away before relenting. "Okay, but one *light* box, deal?"

I took a heavier box than dad realized and headed for my room. "Deal," I called back.

~

Dad arrived in my room a few minutes later, two boxes stacked in his arms. Gunner clearly still intimidated him, and he was going to pay for that show of manliness for days to come. "The rest are at the base of the stairs, kiddo. We can bring them up as we make trips, but this should be a good start towards getting your room put back together."

I looked around my room. It felt like a dream. Like one of the random memories from the games.

It was my room. I wasn't questioning or doubting that fact, but it felt weird seeing it so empty. It was like walking into an old save-file and having to rebuild my surroundings. Yeah, I think in gaming terms a lot, don't I?

So, this is your room? A voice whispered softly in my head.

"Huh?" I turned to look at dad. "Did you say something?"

"You want some help," he asked.

I looked around for a moment before turning and hugging him tightly. I apparently needed to get some sleep. "No thanks, dad. I'm going to make some changes first." I patted the dresser. "New beginnings and all. Maybe I'll even move some furniture around later, if that's okay with you."

Dad nodded. "New beginning and all, eh? I like that." He patted the dresser as well. "Just let me know when you want to move stuff. Neither of us is as strong as we'd like to believe."

15

Jam on It!

Driving, as it turned out, was much more fun than anyone had ever let on. I was a bit of a natural from the word 'go'.

The leather wrapped steering wheel felt like it had been custom-made for my hands, and when I turned the key, the engine roared to life like a grizzly bear woken too early from hibernation. I played with the gas pedal a bit, enjoying the feel of the engine's torque raising the passenger side of the car ever so slightly with each gentle press. It was like the rolling swells of water underneath a surfer waiting to catch the next wave. After a few solid revs, I gave into temptation and pressed the accelerator almost to the floor. I was one with the beast and she was one with me. Together, we would tame the open road like the Lone Ranger and his trusty steed, Silver. My steed, however, was gloss black and sported a good bit of chrome, so maybe Silver wouldn't be appropriate. KITT? No, that's been done.

Knightmare. Yeah, Knightmare was a fitting name for such a noble beast. Dragons would fear her, and other cars would want to be her. For the record, not only dragons would fear her. Like, all the monsters and crap out there would fear her. She's just that badass.

"Knightmare," I said, "let's smoke some pavement!" That means burn rubber, by the way. I don't smoke. Well, only pavement. You know.

I popped in my 8-track of Iron Maiden's *Killers*, pressed the brake pedal, and popped the ratchet shifter into drive. As "The Ides of March" began to throb through my sweet aftermarket speakers, I put the pedal to the metal and rocketed forward, laying a trail of rubber more than 50 feet long.

~

The open road.

The last frontier.

A place where man and beast can roam free of the prying eyes of big brother, big sister, or big they/them. It's a paradise for road warriors and weekend warriors alike. Made famous by the songs of Bruce Springsteen, Golden Earring, The Beach Boys, and The Allman Brothers, and by the movies of Mel Gibson and Chevy Chase, it's a place born of equal parts fantasy and danger.

I was the undisputed master of the domain.

I powered forth like the king of the road I was. A full tank of gas and an empty bladder meant Knightmare and I were an unstoppable force! The sun glinted off my Ray-Ban Wayfarers like an anime villain, and my teeth sparkled like perfect, unblemished porcelain. Nothing could stop me. Nothing could slow me down.

Unfortunately, the police had other plans for my day.

I'd just merged onto Interstate 101 South, when a police cruiser decided my cozy speed of 88 mph looked like too much fun. He turned on his red and blue party-pooper lights. His anti-fun siren blared, cutting into Maiden's groove. When he motioned for me to pull over, I decided to see what his top speed was.

The 101 is a popular scenic highway connecting coastal cities from Ventura, in Southern California, all the way up to the tip-top of Washington State. Highway 1 is an added treat if you really want to take your time, but I'm sure the cops didn't want to join me for a scenic beach tour. Most didn't consider the part of the 101 I was on particularly scenic, but I always enjoyed the views of the San Francisco Bay as I made my way south.

As I nudged the accelerator and increased my speed to a little over 100 mph, the cops poured it on. I knew they were going to give chase. It's what the po-pos do. Chase bad guys. Of course, *I'm* not a bad guy. I'm just out having a bit of fun – on a public thoroughfare, where specific rules and regulations warn against such reckless behavior. But hey, I'm a professional. And Knightmare is no ordinary Sunday-driver. She's got a beast of an engine, suspension that could match the handling of most Italian-made race cars, and puncture-proof tires. Not to mention, I've added a few mods probably not considered street-legal in *any* state. Maybe Wyoming or Montana, they're pretty cool about their motor laws there.

My new friends pulled in so close, I couldn't see the push-guard on the front of the black & white leading the pursuit.

"Well, Knightmare," I said, "let's show 'em what we can do, shall we?"

"Indeed," an ever-so-slightly electronic voice replied. "Any ideas?"

"Keep us in manual drive for now and be ready to take control if I say the safe word." I smirked.

"Sounds like fun," Knightmare chirped.

~

From where I was sitting, the increase from 105 to 165 felt like a long time but watching the two police cars rapidly disappearing in my rearview mirror told a decidedly different story.

"Nice work," I said, patting the steering wheel.

"Teamwork," she responded.

The patrol cars began to creep up again. Apparently, their acceleration wasn't as good as ours, but their top end was better than I'd given them credit for. Fortunately, we'd barely scratched the surface when it came to tricks up the proverbial sleeve. I was just trying to be safe and responsible on a public highway.

"You do realize that 165 mph is neither a safe nor responsible speed," Knightmare commented.

"Hey, they're doing it, too," I replied, pointing behind us.

"Might I suggest taking this to the streets," K.M. interjected. "There's an exit coming up in one and one-half miles.

If you'll permit me to take control for a moment, I've calculated an exit strategy."

"It's all yours, girl." I removed my hands from the wheel, which is not advisable at any speed, let alone 165, and enjoyed the music as my copilot took the wheel.

We were in the fast lane at that point. With the exit fast-approaching, I was anxious to see what Knightmare had in mind.

Just when I was expecting her to slow down, she accelerated! We were approaching the exit at more than 170 mph when she passed a fully loaded eighteen-wheeler. Then, without warning, tires groaning and shock absorbers thumping like the errant bass from my speakers, she shot across two lanes, passing in front of the truck in the process. Once we were clear of the behemoth, she slammed on her brakes. Suddenly, we were in the slow lane, straddling the semi's passenger side.

The police cars shot past the semi, assuming we were still moving along at high speed. As the cops rocketed past the startled truck driver, Knightmare and I cruised leisurely down the off-ramp, turned left, and came to a stop underneath the freeway.

"Police scanners are reporting they've lost the black convertible," K.M. said. She sounded as satisfied as I'd ever heard her sweet little A.I. voice sound. "Where would you like to go next," she asked. "Assuming they continue their search in the direction we were headed, south would be a poor choice."

"Safe assumption," I agreed, taking the wheel. "North it is."

We pulled out from under the freeway, intending to take a left onto the on-ramp leading to the 101 North. I realized right then that I should have turned off the stereo for a minute before leaving our hiding place.

I might have noticed the sound of the police helicopter searching overhead.

~

"It appears we've made a slight miscalculation," Knightmare lamented.

"Nobody's perfect," I said as I course corrected, skipping the on-ramp and choosing a dust covered road leading into a construction site. God bless San Francisco, always construction going on somewhere.

"Speak for yourself," K.M. replied matter-of-factly. "Would you like for me to take control, or will you be the pilot on this ill-advised joyride?"

"I've got this," I replied coolly. "But be ready with the toys, anyway. Since there aren't any civilians where we're going, we can cut loose a bit."

"Understood," Knightmare chirped.

We entered a construction zone at a speed most ATVs would be afraid of. It takes a lot more than speed to frighten Knightmare and me. "Nerves of steel," I said, grinning.

"Technically, I do not have nerves," K.M. commented as I took a hard turn between a dump truck and a loader. "I have a network of neural-based sensors that facilita-"

"I'm well aware," I interrupted. "I built you!" I took another hard left, our tires spitting up dirt and chunks of broken concrete across a mobile home that probably served as an office during working hours. "Do you have any useful information to offer," I asked, trying to be polite.

"The helicopter is still directly overhead," she said, stating the obvious. "There are several police cruisers converging on this location." K.M. paused as I sped between the metal frames of two new buildings. One of them looked like a parking garage. "Sir, we appear to be lost. Would you like me to find a logical escape route?"

I hit the brakes hard, sending dust flying into the air, obscuring us from the view of the chopper overhead.

"I'll take that as a no," Knightmare said with a verbal shrug.

"I've got this," I said, maybe a bit too confidently. Then I slammed the transmission into reverse and accelerated, sending more dust flying in the direction of our pursuer.

"Our current direction puts us on a direct collision course with the approaching police detail," K.M. said, sounding unsure of my sanity.

"I said, I've got this," I repeated. Before she could further question my strategy, I pulled hard on the steering wheel, guiding us into the soon-to-be parking garage.

"This building has no alternate exits," K.M. informed me. "We will be cornered if you insist upon this course of action."

"Ye of little faith," I said as I spun us around and dropped the shifter into drive.

We rocketed forward, bottoming out and sending sparks flying as we hit each incline. As we reached each new floor, we flew several feet into the air, bottoming out again with each landing. I could hear the police sirens echoing through the building. They were inside. My plan had to work.

The police were approaching faster than I expected. They weren't the keystone cops I'd come to expect in cities like Los Angeles or New York. These guys were on the ball.

"The next level is the rooftop," K.M. declared. "I hope you have a plan, or this might be our last hurrah."

"Prepare maneuver Alpha-Zeta," I said, finally.

There was an uncharacteristic pause before Knightmare responded. "Sir, that maneuver has never been tested outside of simulations."

"Well then, it's time for a field test," I shouted as we flew onto the rooftop.

I cranked the wheel hard to the right and began what would either be our last hurrah or our swansong.

~

As I made my way around the perimeter of the rooftop, picking up much-needed speed, the pursuing police cars shot onto the scene. Each one landed hard and sprayed sparks upon impact. They split up as they reached the top and began what the military refers to as a pincer movement, meaning to cut me off from both sides. Like I said, they were good.

But not good enough.

As we hit our final straightaway, the helicopter leveled into sight. Everything was going according to plan.

"Activate Alpha-Zeta, now," I shouted.

Then, several things happened simultaneously.

A rocket booster increased our speed exponentially, sending us crashing through a 4-foot-tall concrete wall, which, by the way, stood no chance against Knightmare's might. As we rocketed through the air, Knightmare initiated an electromagnetic pulse, effectively shutting down all our pursuers' electrical systems. The helicopter was forced to land on the rooftop, amid several useless police cars and many frustrated police officers.

K.M. and I? We crashed through a large plate-glass window on the adjoining building, drove across the floor, which was also under construction, and shot out of the window on the opposite side.

A moment later, we splashed down into the San Francisco Bay.

Oh, yeah, we were safe, too. No sinking or anything to worry about.

You see, Knightmare has more than rocket boosters and E.M.P.s on board. I also outfitted her with an emergency pontoon and hydrofoil system.

James Bond, eat your British heart out.

~

"Packard."

"Yes, Knightmare," I replied groggily.

"Are you feeling okay this morning, son?"

I opened my eyes to find dad standing at the foot of my bed. He looked concerned. "Were you having another nightmare," he asked.

I grinned and rubbed the sleep from my eyes. "Actually, it was a pretty good dream," I replied.

Dad smiled. He was obviously happy to see me content and well-adjusted. He held out his hand, keys dangled from his fingertips. "It's a beautiful day out. I thought maybe it would be

a good time to start your driving lessons."

16
Muscle Memory

Driving, as it turned out, wasn't nearly as much fun as I'd imagined. Although I was a bit of a natural from the word 'go'.

Dad's vinyl wrapped steering wheel felt like he'd crushed and conformed it to fit his hands over many years and miles. When I turned the key, the engine sputtered to life like a temperamental old chihuahua woken too early from a nap. I played with the gas pedal a bit, but dad reminded me it wasn't necessary and was technically bad for the engine.

Oscar the Grouch, the nickname I gave dad's ride, was slow, temperamental, and normally had a pile of trash in the back seat that would have made any auto-detailer cringe. Thankfully, we'd deposited the trash into a receptacle at the Riverboat car wash and dad hadn't had time to toss any fast-food bags, wrappers, or cups over his shoulder since.

We stopped for a bite to eat on our way to Golden Gate Park, where dad mapped out hours of driver's ed fun. The Manor Coffee Shop doesn't have a drive-thru, so we ate in, rescuing Oscar from the prospect of more trash in the back seat.

After a perfectly prepared Denver omelet and an iced coffee, I was ready to take on the world. It was just a shame Oscar didn't have rocket boosters or inflatable pontoons. Oh well, I was sure I'd see my trusty Knightmare in my dreams again. Sooner or later.

~

As I said, I was a natural at the driving thing. Dad was shocked at how easily it came to me.

We tooled around in a large, mostly deserted parking area for about an hour. Once dad was satisfied I had the hang of the basics, he suggested we follow the map of the park he'd so enthusiastically highlighted. The highlights kept us within the confines of the park, but crisscrossed and backtracked enough to give me real world experience with stops, turns, and parking.

We spent another hour or so driving around Golden Gate Park, navigating around real obstacles. We backed up several times, made numerous 3-point turns, and finally parked near the Stow Lake Boathouse where we discussed onboard safety systems until dad realized he was repeating himself.

"Well, dang," dad finally said. "If I didn't know any better, I'd say you started your lessons without me." He smiled proudly. "You're ready for a driver's test and a license, kiddo."

"Really?" I was floored.

"Yeah. You're easily a better driver than I was after an entire year of driving," he admitted. "You sure you've never done this," he joked.

"Only in games," I replied casually.

"Look out," dad suddenly shouted.

I turned my head just in time to see a speeding pickup truck swerve to avoid a group of bicyclists who entered the parking area from a bike path without looking. The truck's course correction put him on a direct collision course with dad's door!

I slammed Oscar into reverse, cranked the wheel, and floored the accelerator. Before dad knew what was happening, we'd backed out of the truck's way and slid sideways into a parallel parking space on the opposite side of the lot.

"Games, huh," he said, still gripping the 'oh, shit handle' over the passenger door.

~

The drive back to good ol' Noe Valley was awkward to say the least. We listened to the *Weirdly Weirdness* podcast, but it was clear we both had other things on our minds. When we pulled into the driveway, obviously distracted by his thoughts, dad shut off the podcast without allowing the episode to finish. That was practically unheard of.

Dad had barely shut off the ignition when he turned to me, clasped his hands together in front of him, and leaned forward slightly. It was awkward talk time. "Games, huh," he said again.

"You said that earlier, dad," I replied. "What do you want me to say?"

"What aren't you telling me," he asked.

"Dad, nothing. I mean, I've only driven in games. Well, dreams, too, but that's it. When else would I have had a chance to learn?"

Dad pursed his lips. "You dream about driving?"

"I've been dreaming about lots of things," I replied.

"Tell me," he said. Then he offered a shrug. "Maybe not out here. Let's go inside."

~

When we got inside, dad got us each a bottle of water and used the restroom. We sat on the couch and I told him about the dreams I'd been having since my return from the brink. Gladiator fights, train robberies, interdimensional invaders, magical quests, space aliens, car chases, and of course, the dreaded dysentery.

Dad's brain was in science mode. He looked like the meme with the facts and figures dropping Matrix-style around the guy's head. The funny dude with the beard, not the cool one. Sorry, dad.

Dad drummed his fingers on his right temple. He was so deep in thought I don't think he was aware of it. "Those are obviously some of the games you've played over the years. Have you had any other dreams," he asked. "About other games, I mean."

"More like random memories that feel real," I said. "But yes. Several of them."

Dad nodded. "I feel like we should go see Irene tomorrow."

I nodded in agreement. "There's something else, dad."

He raised his eyebrows. For a moment, he looked like Mr. Panacharian. "Go ahead," he prompted.

"I really haven't thought much of it, since Irene said my memories would be mixed up for a while anyway."

"Any detail, no matter how seemingly insignificant it might feel, might be important," he said.

"It's going to sound crazy, dad, but I've been seeing and hearing ghosts." Yep, it sounded even more crazy out loud than it had in my head.

Dad just nodded. "It doesn't sound crazy at all, son. I could probably offer a few theories, but I think I'd rather get

Irene's opinion before I start tossing around suppositions. But why don't you tell me a bit about these ghosts anyway. It'll give me time to process some thoughts."

I shrugged. It felt crazy to even mention it, but if it was related, then dad had to know. "The first time was at the Winchester Mystery House. I saw an old cowboy, or an outline of one, twice."

Dad smiled. "Imagine that. A ghost cowboy in the Winchester Mystery House."

"I told you it sounded crazy, dad," I sighed.

"No," he said. "Not at all. Please, continue."

"I've seen others since then," I admitted. "The cowboy keeps showing up when I'm in the bathroom or shower. And then there's a girl. She's shown up in my room a few times, and once in the kitchen. There's more than just them, but they're so hard to make out, dad."

He nodded again, not looking like he doubted me or thought I was the least bit crazy. "And the voices?"

"There's just one voice," I said. "I think it's the girl. She keeps asking questions about the house. It seems like she's trying to get me to answer, but that would just be insane, right?"

"You haven't answered her," dad asked.

"Of course not." I know my expression went sour on that note. "Why would I?"

"To see if she continues on with the conversation," dad suggested.

"Dad, that would be crazy."

"I don't think so." He smiled compassionately. "There's a reason this is happening, and I don't think it has anything to do with your grasp on reality, Packard."

"I don't even know what's real half the time anymore," I lamented.

Dad suddenly brightened up. "Say, you wanna try something? A little experiment in the name of science?"

"Um, sure," I said warily.

Dad hopped up and ran to the hall closet. When he returned, he was holding two unopened rolls of Christmas wrapping paper.

"Oh, no," I said. "Don't tell me we're going to listen to that Arnold Schwarzenegger Christmas album now. What was it called? *Pumping Tinsel?*"

Dad grinned. "Aww, come on, Packard! That's a great album." He tossed me one of the rolls of wrapping paper. "Sadly, no. Christmas is still a few months away, so *Pumping Tinsel* will have to wait." Dad propped his roll on his shoulder, like a batter stepping up to home plate. "Computer," he called out, "play 'Eye of the Tiger'."

Our smart home app replied, "Playing 'Eye of the Tiger' by Survivor, released in 1982," and the song began.

"Defend yourself," dad said loudly, swinging his roll of Evolutants wrapping paper at me wildly.

You could call it instinct, precognition, the Force, but whatever it was, I immediately dropped to one knee and swung my tube over my shoulder. I blocked one of his swipes with that first move and brought my roll around in a new arc that connected with his left ankle with a hollow 'thunk'. If the roll had been solid, I might have hurt him, or at least knocked him down.

"Okay, I yield," dad said, dropping his roll to the floor.

"What was that," I asked, still unsure of what just happened. "How did I do that?"

"Computer," dad called out, "stop the music." The music ceased and dad plopped down on his favorite spot on the couch. "That, son, is muscle memory. The military has been using my tech to acclimate soldiers to all kinds of scenarios over the years, but they still require field training for specific applications. I've never seen it work this way before."

"But I haven't done any of the military programs," I replied. "And I certainly haven't had any field training."

"Not in the traditional sense," dad countered. "But you've had more experience with the indGame simulations than anyone else, ever." He paused, thinking. "And you're the only one with the Arete Nanops coursing through his body. That could be the key."

I was getting anxious. "Can we go see Irene today," I asked.

Dad shook his head. "Not tonight, kiddo. It's been a long day already. We need rest, and considering what we want to talk about, we'd keep Irene up half the night. That wouldn't be very fair to her or George now, would it?"

"I guess not," I conceded.

"We'll go first thing tomorrow, okay," dad asked.

"Okay, dad."

Dad smiled. "Okay then." He picked up the entertainment remote and waved it in front of me. "How's about we order a pizza and watch the new Star Trek?"

"The one with Admiral Kim," I asked.

"Hell yeah," dad replied. "Trekkies have been waiting for this moment for a couple decades."

I nodded enthusiastically. "Make it an all-meat pizza and add a 2 liter of the Dew, and you're on!"

Dad grinned. "Awesome! Go get cleaned up, then." Then dad called out, "Computer, play 'Frosty the Snowman' by Arnold Schwarzenegger."

The smart home app replied, "Playing 'Frosty the Snowman' by Arnold Schwarzenegger, released in 2006," as I ran up the stairs.

I like that song, the voice in my head said softly as I closed my door.

I ignored it. I wasn't ready to answer just yet.

17
Collateral Reality

Dad was true to his word. The next morning, we got an ungodly early start and were in Cupertino by 8:30 am. We found we'd beaten Irene to Arete, so we grabbed a breakfast sandwich and coffee at Dunkies. Dad even grabbed Irene her favorite as a preemptive thanks.

She'd already stopped for coffee, but good ol' Gunner was more than happy to take the extra coffee off dad's hands. He walked off down the hall, humming happily, as we shared the previous day's events with Irene.

Irene listened carefully as dad told her about incidents involving embedded tactile muscle memories, residual ocular echoes, neuro-auditory reverberations, and other phenomena I didn't understand.

"So, Packard," Irene was suddenly observing me like I was a science project. "How do you feel today?"

I thought about it for a moment. "I feel fine, honestly. In fact, I feel great!" I motioned to myself. "I've never felt better."

She smiled and nodded. She was still Irene, not some crazy mad scientist. "Tell me about the ghosts and voices, in your own words, please," she prompted.

"It's like dad said." I shrugged. "I've been seeing shapes and shadows. Some have more definition than others. There's an old cowboy and a girl I can kinda make out, but the rest are just blurs and smudges in the air. Like the special effects in that old movie, *Predator*."

Irene nodded again. It was going to be a question and nodding day. I'd hoped those days were behind us. "How clear are the girl and cowboy? Can you make out what they're wearing? Any facial features?"

"Except for a cowboy hat on the cowboy, clothes aren't visible. And I can make out the girl's hair and some faint details on her face, but that's it," I admitted.

More nodding. "Does either of them look familiar to you?" Irene was jotting notes down, like a therapist.

I thought about that for a moment. "You know? I think so. The cowboy could really be anyone, but I think the girl is Becky."

"Who's Becky," Irene asked, arching an eyebrow.

I'm right here, the voice said in my head.

Dad answered before I could say anything. "She's an NPC in *String Theories.* Do you mean that Becky, Packard?"

I nodded.

Tell them I'm here, the voice said again.

Irene leaned forward, interested. "And the voice? Is that Becky, too?"

Of course it's me, the voice insisted.

"She says yes, it's her," I said sheepishly.

Dad's eyes widened. "You're hearing her right now?"

I nodded again.

Dad looked at Irene. "I told him last night to answer her. What do you think?"

Irene pondered the question for a moment. "Well, I'm not a psychologist, but I don't think it could hurt." She looked at me again. "What do you think, Packard? Are you comfortable answering?"

"It makes me feel like I'm admitting I'm crazy," I replied. "What if she keeps up the conversation? What does that say about me?"

"I get you. Your sanity isn't in question. What's up for evaluation is your physical and emotional responses to the Nanops and full reboot of your brain." Irene paused before continuing, appearing to struggle a bit with her next words. "Packard, when we did what we did, we had no idea if it would work, let alone the long-term ramifications of the process. We had nothing to go on. No previous data extrapolated from trials, no computer simulations, or mathematical predictions, nothing. It was a spur of the moment idea that thankfully worked, but we were running into a minefield wearing a blindfold and snowshoes."

I know I should have laughed at the analogy, but my anxiety levels were well outside the humor range. "So, answer her," I asked, looking between her and dad. Neither one looked particularly confident in an answer.

"Yes," Irene answered finally. "Please tell us what she says, if anything."

So are you finally going to answer me, then, she asked.

"Yes," I replied, feeling stupid as hell.

Well then, it's nice to finally talk to you, she said.

"She said it's nice to talk to me," I told dad and Irene.

Dad motioned for me to continue talking, like I was having an actual conversation.

"It's um, nice, uh, talking to you, too," I stammered. I never stammer unless I'm talking to a girl.

Is that a question or a statement, Pack?

"Uh, a statement. Definitely a statement," I said, almost forgetting I was talking to myself.

Well, good then, she said. *So, what're we doing here? And who's the lady?*

"Uh, she wants to know why we're here," I told them. To Irene I added, "and who *you* are."

"Tell her then," they both said.

"Hey, can you tell me something first," I asked.

Anything.

"Who are you," I asked.

Seriously? She sounded offended. *You don't know?*

I looked at dad and Irene, not really knowing where else to look while I spoke to a voice only I could hear. "Becky?"

Bingo-des, she said happily. *Are you okay, Pack? Is this a doctor's office?*

"Uh, yeah, kind of. Her name is Irene. She's dad's, um, our friend."

Irene smiled at the comment.

"She's, uh, helping with a problem I've got."

But are you okay, the Becky-voice asked again.

"Yeah, I think so." I was feeling really uncomfortable by that time. "Hey, Becky, do you mind if we continue this conversation later? Irene's probably got a busy day ahead of her. Dad and I dropped in on her unannounced."

Well, that was rude of you guys. Speaking of rude, thanks for not offering me any pizza last night.

"You were there," I asked.

I was sitting right next to you the whole time, she said, sounding offended again. *It's about time Harry Kim got some love. Next, we need Travis Mayweather to get his own ship.*

I shrugged at dad and Irene. "She's a hardcore Trekkie," I said, dumbfounded.

"Of course she is." Dad grinned. "I wrote her code."

Oh, and tell your dad that aside from not offering me any pizza, he's pretty cool, Becky offered. *My dad ran off with a cocktail waitress when I was little, so it was nice to see you two interacting like a father and son who actually like each other.*

"He's alright," I replied.

Dad put up his hand questioningly.

"She said you're nice, even though you didn't offer her any pizza," I said.

Dad smiled. "I'll be a better host next time."

"She also said her dad left when she was a little girl, so I should appreciate you." I shrugged.

Dad's smile dropped. "She said that? Did she say anything else about that?"

"About you?" I didn't see how that really mattered. "I appreciate you-"

"No," dad interrupted. "About her father."

"Just that he ran off with a cocktail waitress or something," I replied. "Why? Does that matter?"

Dad looked shaken. Irene put a hand on his shoulder. "Hal, are you okay," she asked softly.

Dad looked from Irene, to me, then back to Irene. "That was part of Becky's backstory, but it's never mentioned anywhere in the game."

"So Packard read it somewhere? In your notes, maybe," Irene asked.

Dad shook his head slowly. "Not possible. I never wrote it down. I decided it was a little on the dramatic side and not important to the story, so the idea never left my head."

~

Following our debriefing, the four of us – I'm including Becky now too, since she wouldn't leave me alone – went into what Irene called a nanoperating room. It was a laboratory that made me rethink the mad scientist evaluation. There were monitors, headsets, scanners, and portable tool carts surrounding what looked like a dentist's chair at the center of the room.

The only things missing were giant electrodes and a way to raise me into a lightning storm like Frankenstein's monster.

Irene could see me scanning the room nervously. "Are you ready for your Novocaine," she asked.

I turned with a start, only to find her smiling.

"I'm only kidding," she said. "The worst thing we'll do here today is draw a little blood. Nothing we haven't done before."

I was still apprehensive about what I was looking at. "Then why all the sciencey stuff?"

Becky said out loud what dad and Irene's expressions were saying. *Really? I just joined this party, and even I don't have to ask that question.*

I laughed. "Ha... just kidding." I gestured towards the chair. "Shall I uh, just take a seat, then?"

"Please," Irene replied. "Hal, would you mind strapping him in?"

I turned to look at her again. She was smiling. Thank God.

"Just kidding," she said through her smile.

"Touché," I said back, a bit sourly.

Dad took a seat in a far less comfortable-looking chair as I reclined in a cushioned, form fitting medieval torture device. "Don't fall asleep, kiddo," he said, looking like he was ready to nod off himself.

"Not a chance," I said, still eying the equipment surrounding me suspiciously. "Becky won't give me a moment of silence, anyway."

I thought you liked talking to me, she said. *I like talking to you.*

"It's not that," I replied. "I've just got a lot on my mind right now."

Dad opened his eyes and looked at me weird. "Huh?"

Irene responded for me. "I think he's talking to Becky."

The mention of Becky bothered dad.

Tell Irene thank you for acknowledging me, Becky said. *You should have told me that before, Pack. Do you mind if I just stay here with you quietly?*

"Becky said to thank you for acknowledging her, Irene," I said. "And, no, I don't mind, Becky. For the record, I like talking to you."

Irene looked around the room. I think she was beginning to wonder if Becky was a real ghost. "You're welcome, Becky," she said finally.

Becky was quiet for a moment before speaking again. *Hey Pack, I didn't want to ask, but what's happening here? I know nobody can see me, and only you can hear me. Am I dead? I'm not going to lie, I'm scared.*

"Me too," I replied. "I'll tell you what. You stay here with us, and we'll figure out what's going on together. Okay?"

Okay.

"And when we get home, maybe we can have a slice of cold pizza together?" I was trying to sound positive.

Woah, slow down there, lover-boy, she chided, making me happy dad and Irene couldn't hear her.

I wasn't sure what to say to that. "I, uh, that's not–"

I could hear her giggling.

"Oh, I see. Everybody's a comedian today." I forgot dad and Irene were in the room. "You have a nice laugh."

Pack? She sounded frightened, despite the giggles.

"Yeah?"

Thank you for letting me stay. And pizza with you and your dad sounds amazing.

I opened my mouth to respond, but Becky cut me off.

Now would be a good time to stop while you're ahead.

~

Several hours, countless uncomfortable procedures, and a blood-test later, Irene pulled up a stool in front of me and plopped a stack of papers down on one of the tool carts.

"So," I asked, "do I know Kung Fu?"

The joke, while lost on Irene, made dad and Becky laugh.

"To be honest, the driving might be a fluke," she replied. "It would be a mistake to make any unsubstantiated assumptions at this juncture."

"What about the sword fighting," dad asked.

That was really badass, Becky interjected. She'd been quiet for most of the tests, so I totally forgot she was there. Outta sight, outta mind, right?

Irene shrugged. "I'm not ruling your theory out, Hal. But I'm not ready to put a ring on it, either." She picked up the stack of papers and thumbed through. "Your test results are phenomenal, Packard. Completely unprecedented, and totally unexpected. Your brain activity is off the charts." She held up one of the printouts showing a series of separate top-down, color scans of my brain. The colors were all over the place. There were electric shades of blue, red, yellow, green, and every possible combination. They looked like Picasso had colored Easter eggs. "I produced an overlay of the fMRI and EEG results. It's my best tool to illustrate what's going on."

Dad stood up and joined us. He looked impressed by the printout. "In my years developing the NR systems, I've seen a lot of brain scans. I've never seen anything like this."

I looked at them, wondering if I should be worried about anything I was seeing.

Irene pointed at the grid of images. "Our tests highlight areas of activity in the brain. Certain regions should light up, depending on what we were discussing, what questions I was asking, etcetera." She paused for a moment, probably for dramatic effect. "What do you see here?"

Dad answered before I could. "Everything looks like it's lit up, everywhere. *All the time.*"

"I was hoping Packard would answer that," Irene said, "but, yes. That's exactly what we're seeing."

"Is that bad," I asked.

Becky asked the same thing quietly.

Irene nodded. Not what I wanted to see. "It can be if it continues this way. Neurons in the brain interact by sending each other chemical messages. Gamma-aminobutyric acid normally restrains neural activity, preventing neurons from getting too trigger-happy and firing off too many stimuli. You're producing it, but it's not enough to keep up with the massive amounts of data your brain is trying to sort through. My concern is that abnormally increased activity in the hippocampus and prefrontal cortex can impair memory and attention over time."

"How much time," I asked.

Irene shook her head again. The day was full of good news. "Nobody knows. We're dealing with unprecedented activity."

Dad asked the question already on the tip of my tongue. "When you say memory and attention impairment, what kind of effects are we talking about, long-term?"

"Worst case? Schizophrenia, cognitive decline, and early onset Alzheimer's, to name a few. Before we start panicking here, let me say I'm a bad news first girl." She tapped the pile of papers. "There's a lot of good news in this pile as well."

"Hasn't anyone told her she's supposed to ask which news you want before just tossing it at you like a live grenade," Becky asked.

Irene raised an eyebrow, and dad looked around the room comically.

"Did they just *hear* me," Becky asked, sounding embarrassed.

"Becky, I presume," Irene said, looking like she'd just stepped into the *Twilight Zone.*

"Um, hi," Becky replied.

Dad stumbled backwards and fell into the chair he'd been sitting in a few moments earlier. "Hello, Becky."

"Hi Mr. Campbell. Nice to meet you."

Dad looked around the room, feeling what I'd already been feeling for a while.

"Hard to know where to look, isn't it," I asked.

Dad nodded slowly as the *Twilight Zone* theme played in my head.

"Hey, Becky." I had a weird thought. "What song's playing in my head right now?"

A moment of silence followed, and I assumed she was listening. "How would I know? I'm not a mind reader. Oh, sorry about the comment, Miss Irene."

Irene managed a smile through the look of abject shock that had taken over her face. "It's Irene Chow, Becky, but Irene is just fine."

"I'll stick with Mr. Campbell," dad said absently.

"Now that we've all been introduced," I said, "would anybody object to moving on to the good news?"

~

"Sorry Becky," I said. "I didn't mean to act like this was unimportant. I know you're scared and confused too. Maybe even more than me. But if we're gonna figure out what's going on, I know Irene's our best bet. I wasn't trying to be dismissive. I just have the feeling that whatever's happening in my brain ties into your appearance. So, since we were already figuring my issues out, two birds, one stone, right?"

"Yeah. I am scared, and really confused," Becky replied. "But you're right. I'm sorry I interrupted, Irene."

"It's okay," Irene said. "I understand you're frightened. You have every right to be. Both of you." She fidgeted with the papers for a moment before continuing. "Until I heard your voice, I was ready to dismiss you as a hallucination, a very elaborate one, but still just that. Now, I have to accept and include a completely unknown factor into what we're dealing with. When I say we, I mean you too."

"Where do we even start," dad croaked.

Back to the head shaking. Irene was clearly in uncharted territory. "Well, let me tell you what's encouraging first. Then we can move on to the new matters at hand."

Dad and I agreed. We could even hear a small, begrudging grunt of acceptance from Becky.

"Some of this might not sound like good news on the surface," Irene began, "but I'll address all of it, and explain why it's not necessarily *bad*." She started to look through the pages when she stopped, leaving the one she'd stopped on hidden from sight. "Packard, would you mind closing your eyes for a moment?"

"Sure." I closed my eyes, tipping my face to the ceiling for good measure.

I heard the pages rustle again before Irene finally spoke. "Becky, can you tell me what the highlighted words on this page say?"

"Subject exhibits increased amygdala volume," Becky replied without a moment's hesitation.

"You can open your eyes, Packard," Irene told me. "It all seems so unreal, but, as the Monkees once said, I'm a believer."

Dad's expression was sufficiently dumbfounded.

"Wasn't that Smash Mouth," Becky asked.

"You're both right," I said a bit harshly. "What does that even mean, Irene? Because that doesn't sound good at all."

"Increased amygdalic volume is common in children with unusually high levels of anxiety. Basically, the amygdala is a communications hub between the parts of the brain that process incoming signals and the parts that interpret those signals. In your case, it makes sense. The influx of memories and your brain's inability to distinguish between explicit and implicit memories is repeatedly pushing your mental panic button. As with everything else, your basal ganglia are lit up like a Christmas tree."

"That's also a sign of increased anxiety, right," Becky asked.

Irene raised an eyebrow, a clear sign she was impressed. "Somebody's been paying attention in their anatomy classes. Couple that with elevated levels of cortisol and adrenaline, and bam, you've got stress. Packard, your brain is strong and healthy, just overworked, and overprotective. It's in 'just in case' mode." Irene pointed at the colored brains again. "Your hippocampus, which is named after seahorses, by the way, not hippos," she said, looking directly at me.

She'd headed me off at the joke-pass. "I wasn't going to say anything," I said with just the slightest hint of guilt.

Irene narrowed her eyes and smiled thinly. "Uh huh. Anyway, the hippocampus encodes events into memories, deals with flashbacks, fills in deficits, and sorts through memory fragments. It also deals with the formation, organization, and storage of new memories. Every potential memory has to pass through the poor hippocampus several times for evaluation and to make future associations." She looked at me with what was probably pity. "Kiddo, your hippocampus needs a vacation, badly."

"You have no idea," I sighed. "Disneyland, anyone?"

"Oh my gosh, yes," Becky replied excitedly.

Irene ignored the exchange. "Back to the basal ganglia. Rather than putting it all on the hippocampus, motor learning occurs in other brain areas – the basal ganglia and cerebellum. When you were sick, your basal ganglia were the first areas of your brain affected, making walking and other motor skills impossible. The fact that they're performing beyond normal peak expectations isn't simply good, it's freaking phenomenal. The Nanops fully restored their function and then some." Irene looked between dad and me. "Any questions? Comments? Becky?"

Dad and I shook our heads. Though I really needed coffee to continue, I felt we'd already interrupted Irene enough.

Becky replied, "no, ma'am."

"Okay, then I have more good news. There are two types of long-term memory; semantic, which is knowledge about the self, and episodic, which is event-specific knowledge related to past personal experiences. Your brain seems to be recognizing the differences between those types of memories very nicely. You know who you are, and that goes a long way towards a good outcome. What your brain is having trouble distinguishing, is the difference between episodic memories from real life and the games."

"Okay, now you've lost me," Becky interrupted.

"Dad and I will explain that later, I promise," I said. "Okay?"

"Alright," came the disembodied voice.

Irene nodded, satisfied. "I believe you consciously understand the difference between the two sets of memories. Your subconscious is just trying to catch up. Once it does, the increased activity should start to taper off, starting with your amygdala, then your limbic system, and finally the whole shebang."

I wanted to razz her for her usage of the word shebang, but I was still feeling too anxious for playful banter. "Why is my brain confused between the memories," I asked.

"It's a combination of two things. The first is cognitive boundaries, which are like cut scenes in movies. Let's face it, memories are basically just a weird series of cut scenes. Imagine a scene where someone opens a door and walks through. Normally, the scene would cut to the person on the other side of the door. That's a soft boundary. Your brain can easily make sense of that. A hard boundary occurs when the second scene is completely unrelated to the first, like a crazy music video with a bunch of random scenes coming at you rapid-fire. Essentially, your brain is watching an endless music video with mostly hard boundaries. The good news is, just like with a hard drive, your brain will eventually sort all the data and put it into a more logical order."

"You said there were two factors," dad said, looking like he needed coffee as much as I did. "What's the other one?"

"Sorry," Irene said. "The second is experience dependent neuroplasticity, which means every experience we're exposed to has the capacity to strengthen our brain. I believe your brain is dealing with everything in a logical and rational manner, in the order it should. You can't expect to filter a swimming pool's worth of water as fast as you could filter a glass of water, would you?"

I shook my head.

"Your memories are no different. We added a lifetime's worth of memories to your brain. Without any precedents set, we expected your mind to integrate them immediately. That was clearly an unreasonable expectation, hon."

"You're right," I said. "That does make me feel a little better."

"Me too," dad chimed in.

"I'm still completely in the dark," Becky said, frustration apparent in her voice.

"Dad and I will explain everything when Irene's done," I said.

"Promise," Becky asked.

"Yeah," dad said before I could. "You have our word."

Becky sighed. It was like a delicate breeze in the room. "Thank you."

Irene smiled at the exchange, but mostly smiled at dad. She was clearly a fan of his parenting style. She looked back at me. "So, kiddo. What we need to do next is develop an outlet for you."

I must have looked confused.

"Exercise," she said. "You need to burn off excess energy to bring your brain chemistry back under control."

I showed her my skinny arms and bird-legs. "I haven't done much exercising in the past half-decade, Irene," I lamented.

"I can help with that," a voice said from the doorway. It was Gunner. "If you need to exercise, we've got a gym here on site. I'd be happy to train you."

"Wow, thank you," I said. "That's really cool."

"No problem, kid." He nodded towards my left side. "If she'd like, your girlfriend can join us too."

"My *wha-*" I turned to see Becky standing beside me, looking just like the last time I saw her in Laboratory 311, minus the enviro-suit. My jaw dropped.

"His *wha-* You can *see* me?" Becky was as shocked as I was.

But nobody was quite as shocked as dad.

Gunner lurched forward and caught him when he fainted.

LEVEL THREE
POWER UPS

18
Making New Friends

Once dad came to, he, Becky, and I relocated to a boardroom, and had a crazy heart-to-heart-to-heart conversation. I have to say, Becky took the idea of potentially being a fictional NPC much better than I would have. The bizarre thing we kept coming back to, though, is that Becky knew stuff I didn't. And there was absolutely zero explanation for her physical presence.

Irene was still working on my blood test results, but aside from the idea that the Nanops were somehow responsible for Becky's appearance, which seemed to be the most likely explanation, we were grasping at straws.

She was a thinking, reasoning, physical being with fears, likes, and dislikes. She felt frustration and anger, and when I put my hand on hers to comfort her, she felt like a human being. I had no reason to believe otherwise.

She even took off her sweater while we were talking because she was too hot. Tell me that's not 100% human.

Thankfully, Gunner brought her an Arete NanoPhys tee shirt to change into. Unlike the world of *String Theories*, we did have to err on the side of modesty. Besides, we didn't need dad fainting again.

For all our uncertainty, Becky insisted she had a life and memories before she got 'stuck' in our world. There was no argument dad or I could offer to refute her claims.

She was genuinely sad when we told her about losing my mom so young, and she welled up with real tears at the story about my illness and impending death. She hugged dad when he cried while telling her about the accident and my brain-death.

"I don't know what's happening, Mr. Campbell," Becky said softly, "and I don't know if what you and Irene did somehow brought me here, but I'm glad you did what you did. The world's a better place with Packard in it."

I was dumbstruck by her words, and dad, well, he finally lost it. His sobs rivaled the day I came back to life.

"Please," he sighed once he'd stopped the waterworks. "Just call me Hal."

~

Shortly after we finished our conversation, dad had four large pizzas delivered to the facility. He and I were famished, but Becky ate like she'd been lost at sea for months. Even Gunner, who was a calorie burning machine, was impressed by her ability to make the slices disappear like a bounty hunter into a sarlacc pit.

Irene, who was lactose intolerant, took a pill before partaking in the glory of pizza. Dad needed to write those pills into *Animehem*. Santa's legendary emissions made it a moral imperative.

"The rest of your blood work came back," Irene informed me between bites. "It was just as we suspected. The Nanop activity is through the roof." She took another bite. After washing it down with a hearty swig of water, she continued. "The Nanops are in all your systems. They've essentially fused with every aspect of your physiology. Your relationship with them is 100% symbiotic now. They rely on you as much as you rely on them."

"Fused?" I cringed a bit. "That sounds ominous, I'm not going to lie." I already felt desensitized to the craziness that came with the majority of our conversations, but 'fused' carried a dark wave of finality with it.

"Think of them as super-powered antibodies, if that helps," Irene offered. "So far, we've seen nothing to suggest that they've been anything but beneficial..." She trailed off and looked at Becky curiously. "And yet, you're here."

"The elephant in the room, huh?" Becky picked up another slice of pizza. "I feel like my being here throws a wrench into all your possible explanations."

Irene and dad both nodded.

"I'd like to run the tests I did on Packard on you," Irene said. "Would that be okay with you?"

Becky nodded, opting not to talk with her mouth full. After swallowing the bite she was working on, she responded. "Whatever you have to do, I'm in." She paused for a moment. "It's not like I have a choice, though, right?"

Dad spoke up. "You might not have chosen to be here, but you'll always have choices now that you are. Nothing happens against your will."

"He's right," Irene agreed. "But any help you can offer would be appreciated."

"Nope, I'm all in," Becky declared with the same unwavering courage I witnessed in Laboratory 311.

"You two kids are brave," Gunner said, licking pizza grease off his fingers. "I'd be a basket case if I was in your shoes."

Becky laughed. "If you were in my shoes, your feet would be sore."

We all laughed at that, and Gunner clapped both of us on the backs. "I'm glad Irene's letting me help out with you two."

I looked up at Gunner and smiled. "I'm glad you're on our side. I'd hate to be one of your enemies."

Gunner laughed. "Who? Me?" He twisted his face comically. "I'm as harmless as a kitten."

"I find that hard to believe," Becky laughed. Then she looked at me and grinned. "Then again, looks can be deceiving."

"Well, I'm done eating," Irene told her, as if on cue. "Anytime you're ready, I'm good to go."

Becky stood and stretched. She glanced around the room, looking for something but clearly not finding it. "Can I use a restroom first?"

"I can show you where it is," Gunner offered.

Irene got up and walked with them towards the hall. "I'll be back in the nanoperating room when you're done. Just meet me there."

And then, just like that, dad and I were alone again.

Dad shifted uncomfortably in his seat. "So, what do you think, kiddo," he asked. "Is she an NPC come to life somehow, a strange visitor from another world, or something else?"

"I've been thinking about that the whole time," I admitted. "I don't think she came out of my head, dad. If she did, how would she know stuff only you knew? Unless you have Nanops in you, somehow?"

Dad shook his head and yawned. "That's good deductive reasoning, Packard. Truthfully, I offered to let Irene test them out on me first, but your situation was critical. We had no time for preparation. Not to mention, she needed me to manage the file system and quantum upload. If things went even remotely sideways, I might not have been able to help with your procedure."

"Makes sense," I agreed. "Honestly, dad, I'm stumped. What about you? Any insights or wild theories?"

When he didn't answer, I turned to find he'd finally nodded off in one of the big, leather boardroom chairs. I had to admit, they were comfortable.

I watched the hallway and listened to dad saw logs for a few minutes. When Gunner and Becky passed by, headed back towards the nanoperating room, I tipped my chair back and curled

up into a ball like the world's biggest kitten.

19

Assassins Inc.

College. The adventure of a lifetime. The place where you establish lifelong friendships, develop career goals, do things you'll never talk to your parents or kids about, and rack up massive amounts of student debt.

Yep, well, two out of four ain't bad, right?

Actually, one of those didn't count. Kyle was my only friend, and I'd known him since kindergarten.

The student debt, though? I had that down pat. If there's a science to racking up debt, I should have a doctorate in it already.

As for those things we'd never share with anyone we'd hope to have respect us in the future? I was about to catch up on that particular bell curve in a big way.

No, I wasn't doing drugs. That's not my thing. But I was going to need protection.

Hey, get your mind out of the gutter! I needed Kevlar, not Latex. Kyle and I were about to kill someone.

Don't get the wrong idea now. We weren't serial killers or murderers or anything. We had recently established ourselves as contract killers, paid assassins for hire. And no, it's not the same thing as a murderer. We were going to be taking out the trash. Like The Punisher, or John Wick, *righteous vigilantes.*

Pack and Kyle.

The trash men.

~

You might wonder how a couple of nice guys like us could get mixed up in such a dirty business.

Remember the crippling student debt I mentioned? Yeah, that was reason enough.

It all started a couple of months earlier. Kyle and I both received some bad news. My news was a bit of a mixed bag, but we'll get to that in a moment.

Both of us discovered our funding was getting cut off. Kyle had spent the better part of four years playing video games and repeating classes multiple times instead of advancing into anything useful. His parents finally decided that an education was not anything that would ever benefit their wayward son and pulled the plug on what he'd assumed was an eternal cash-flow to keep him out of their hair. Boy was he wrong. Other than playing games, Kyle had zero life skills. He couldn't cook, wouldn't clean, and didn't know anything about Star Wars, DC Comics, or Dungeons and Dragons. He had nothing to offer anyone. But he was my friend, and if nothing else, I'm loyal.

My bad news was also due to loss of funding, but it was more of a bureaucratic thing. I didn't have wealthy parents, but somehow the government decided they made too much anyway and denied my aid. I had already racked up tens of thousands of dollars in debt, and it was just going to get worse.

Backing up a bit. A week before all that happened, I received a call from an attorney in Montana who represented my crazy uncle Jack. Jack was one of those 'doomsday preppers' you read about. He'd bought property in Montana in the 1980s and had been completely off the grid, and his rocker, ever since. Over the years, he'd amassed an impressive, mostly legal assortment of survival gear and weapons. But as holds true with many things, Jack's paranoia didn't amount to anything. He died alone in his Montana compound, surrounded by cinder blocks, canned beans, and guns and ammo, instead of his loved ones.

The attorney, Cyrus Montgomery Nelson, a Montana lawyer's name if ever I heard one, said I was the sole heir to Uncle

Jack's estate. The estate was a rundown patch of scrub brush a few miles north of Jordan, Montana. The property had a 1970s era RV on it, which Uncle Jack had parked there more than 30 years earlier, and never started again. There were a few tool sheds full of black widows and God only knew what else, and an underground fallout shelter, where Jack spent the last few years of his life. According to ol' Cy, as the attorney asked me to call him, the fallout shelter was a virtual treasure trove of home defense wares and apocalypse-proof goodness. Kyle, who was honestly lost without a video game controller in his hand, took a bit of convincing to join me on a road trip to Montana and back. I finally won him over by offering him his pick of the guns at ol' Jack's ranch. One gun for the promise of a copilot and the use of his car. Yeah, Kyle has a car, too. One of those electric hybrids. Did I mention his folks were rich? But as you already know, he screwed that pooch royally. I'll be the first to say, Kyle had a sweet deal until he didn't.

You're probably wondering, *why trade for the gun?* Well, I had no wheels, and no other friends I was aware of. Kyle was my Obi-Wan Kenobi, my only hope.

His favorite genre of video game just so happened to be the first-person shooter. He was always bragging he was a better shot than a special forces sniper, so the temptation of having an actual tool of his fictional trade was too much for even the mighty Kyle to resist.

My partner in crime slyly negotiated some energy drinks and Doritos into the deal, and we finally embarked upon the road trip that put us on a collision course with destiny.

~

The road trip, while long, was mostly uneventful. I did all the driving, as I realized that, while Kyle was a veritable Mario Andretti in games like *Jam on It!*, his driving in the real world was more comparable to my Grandma Florence's skill levels and highway speeds.

In between listening to Kyle's playlist, which seemed to include multiple instances of every version of "Holiday Road" ever recorded, I told him about my childhood summers spent in Montana with Uncle Jack. It was really no surprise that I'd never talked about those summers to anyone. Uncle Jack wasn't abusive, not in the ways most people define it, anyway. But if you can honestly tell me forcing a six-year-old to beat obstacle courses meant to make marines cry isn't abuse, then we probably grew up very differently. For all the drills my dad's older brother put me through, I ended up being a flaming pacifist. To this day, I'm still terrified of guns.

I'm not sure Uncle Jack would have left me all his toys if he'd known I was just going to end up selling them for college tuition. According to Cy, though, I was the only family member Jack had any redeeming memories of. He and my dad hadn't seen eye to eye in years, and their sister, my aunt Ruth, had moved to Japan with her husband when he'd been transferred there by the Air Force.

I was it. Imagine, me, somebody's favorite nephew.

~

My late uncle's property was a hell of a lot more than just scrub brush. And frankly, it was a lot bigger than I had remembered, despite me being a lot smaller the last time I'd set foot on it. Using the keys Cy overnighted me, we accessed the compound through a large rolling gate. A 10-foot-tall electric fence protected the three land-locked sides of the ranch. Hell Creek, which was more of a small river, ran right along the northern border of the land, and was protected by multiple coils of barbed wire held up by a series of crisscrossed timbers. I wouldn't have been surprised to find landmines buried along the shoreline.

Yeah, hard pass on a stroll along the riverside.

The old obstacle courses were still there, some of which ran through the creek, offering an icy version of the land-based runs. Sandpits dotted the tree-lined terrain, each one adorned with some sort of structure to climb over or crawl under. Knotted ropes hung strategically from trees like vines in a Tarzan film. Each one offered the chance for a climb or a swing, but none had a tire tied to the end. Uncle Jack had no time for silliness.

Kyle lit up when he saw the shooting range, but I reminded him we were on a tight schedule, which did not allow for Neanderthalic activities. We were there to collect whatever we could fit into his car, and head back to campus before classes resumed three days later. Kyle protested as hotly as his lazy ass would dare, but finally gave up with a huff, promising to never let me use his chosen weapon on the rifle range when we got home.

Frankly, I would have been just fine if I never had to handle another weapon, nurse my ringing ears, or smell burnt gunpowder on my fingers ever again. But that was not to be. Otherwise, we wouldn't have much of a story now, would we?

The RV Jack lived in at one time had been relegated to little more than a huge filing cabinet. Inside, Kyle and I found hundreds of stacked, white file boxes with titles scrawled on the sides in black magic marker. Some were boring, some were cryptic, and some, like the 'Area 51', 'Bermuda Triangle/Land's End South Carolina Connection', 'Regress Virus', and 'Kennedy Assassination' files were worthy of a raised eyebrow.

"Should we take any," Kyle wondered aloud.

I shook my head. "No, not on this trip. We can come back some day. This place is mine now, bro." I stopped for a moment, considering how much Kyle had helped me and how ungrateful I'd been acting. "If you'd like, once we get our finances in order, we can come back during a break and dig in deeper."

Kyle beamed. "Can we come shoot my gun?"

"Only if you run the obstacle courses first," I replied, barely keeping a straight face.

Kyle frowned. "You're kind of a dick. You know that?"

I laughed. "Sorry man. Yeah, shooting would be fine. Just don't ask me to hold the gun, okay?"

Kyle smirked, forgetting about the obstacle course. "More ammo for me, then," he replied smugly.

We saved the underground bunker for last, as we expected to spend the most time there.

Cy might have undersold the rest of the property's potential, but when he called the bunker a treasure trove, he'd been spot-on. Crates stacked upon crates of guns, ammo, emergency rations, and survival supplies obscured the entire northern wall. Many of the crates bore the logo of 'Preppa Pig', a huge, online survival supply store. It seems Uncle Jack was one of their biggest customers.

Across from the crates was a wall of computer equipment and old-school radio gear. We obviously failed to notice the multitude of security cameras as we explored. A bank of small color monitors clearly showed the entire compound from every angle imaginable, including underwater surveillance in Hell Creek. Uncle Jack was ready for everything, up to and including World War Three.

"You know there's no way we're getting all this into my car," Kyle groaned. "Even if we did, the suspension isn't made for this kind of weight."

"Yeah, you're right," I said, looking around. Then, something caught my eye. More keys.

On the wall, just inside the doorway at the base of the stairs we'd entered from, was a set of hooks and what looked like car keys.

A closer inspection confirmed my suspicion. Two sets of keys, one labeled 'Winnebago', and the other 'Bronco', hung side by side, closest to the door. There were also keys for a well pump, generator, fuel reserve, and solar batteries. World War Three had nothing on Uncle Jack.

"Who was this guy," Kyle marveled, looking around the bunker in awe.

There was a dusty picture frame on the wall next to the keys. I pulled it down, not expecting what it contained. I held out the frame for Kyle to see.

"Is that you, bro," he asked, looking at the comically grinning child standing next to the lanky, bearded man.

"Yeah, that was me," I said softly.

Kyle looked around the room. "Bro, you realize this is the only picture in this place, right?"

I'd noticed. "Yeah. I'm not sure what to make of it." I shrugged.

"I guess he loved you, dude," Kyle said, almost sounding sentimental. "Dang, you were small!" He laughed, ruining what was almost a moment.

"I was like six," I laughed. "Of course I was small."

~

As it turned out, the RV wasn't the clunker Cy believed it to be. Uncle Jack was, if nothing else, the consummate prepper. Everything he had on his ranch was useful and in good working condition, including the RV, and an old, army green '60s Bronco hidden underneath an equally green tarp behind Jack's rolling home.

It took Kyle and me most of the day to move the file boxes from the RV to the bunker. We spent a good bit of the night moving as many crates up into the RV as we could safely fit. Kyle wisely recommended leaving a path to the bathroom and fridge, though in the spirit of using space wisely, we'd blocked the side door. Our only remaining access to the back of the beast was through the gap between the front captain's chairs. We didn't mind, though. We'd accomplished our mission. There was enough artillery on board to overthrow a small country.

Before we hit the road, Kyle suggested we requisition some food from the 10' x 10' area Jack cordoned off as the kitchen. The kitchen's design proved my uncle was as industrious as he was paranoid. He stacked crates of food, seeds, and anything related to not dying of thirst or starvation, to create the walls and counters of his makeshift galley. Enough cookware for one hung carefully on the wall above a propane stove, and sitting next to the large, aluminum sink, were two sets of dishes and utensils.

The second set was what got to me. It was a small child's set of Team Rex dishes and utensils. The ones I used when I visited. They were stacked neatly next to a larger, well-worn set

Jack used every day of his life in that bunker. *I guess he loved you, dude.* Kyle's words hit me like a freight train.

I turned to Kyle, who was busy putting canned foods into a box. "I'm taking a case of bottled water up to the RV. Then I'll hook the Jeep up to the tow bar on the back." I looked around before setting the keys to the bunker next to the box Kyle was filling. "Lock up when you're done, will you?"

"Will do, bro," Kyle replied. Kyle was humming the theme music to the Mike Ferrari video game series. He was like a savant when it came to those games. Like he was born to be in them. Thankfully, he didn't see my expression when I walked away from the dishes. I didn't need him thinking I needed consoling or anything. I was just feeling a bit, well, nostalgic, and I wasn't really accustomed to that emotion.

~

A few minutes later, Kyle brought out some canned and boxed foods, but forgot a can opener. I sent him back to find one while I finished hooking the Bronco up to the rear of the RV.

Kyle returned with a small bag and set it in his car. "Anything else," he asked.

"Yeah." I nodded, my expression exaggeratedly grim. "Take a leak behind one of those trees over there before we leave. We don't want to stop more than we have to."

Kyle nodded at the tree directly behind me. It was closer than the others I suggested. "What's wrong with that one," he asked.

"It's already been fertilized," I replied, hooking up the taillight relays to the Bronco.

"Gross," Kyle muttered as he headed to the recommended line of trees.

Shortly after Kyle's potty break, we got on the road.

The drive back was slow-going, but steady. Kyle followed me closely, making sure the Bronco was safe and keeping any nosey police cars from getting behind me. We really didn't want to risk getting pulled over with a paramilitary's worth of weapons and ammo in the back of an old RV. I can just imagine my parent's reaction. They could quote Oppenheimer while they rained destruction down on my poor little head.

That would be a no bueno.

I imagined Kyle behind me, happily moving at grandpa speed, thanks to the RV, and be-bopping along, listening to his endless stream of "Holiday Road" inspired tunes.

I, on the other hand, discovered a handful of old cassettes in the RV's glove compartment. While the assortment mostly consisted of old country music, like Jerry Reed, Charlie Pride, and Merle Haggard, I was pleased to find some more upbeat stuff, like Fleetwood Mac, Steely Dan, Chuck Mangione, and Chicago. There was even a cassette of the old *Saturday Night Fever* soundtrack, which I suspected someone else had left in the RV way back in the '80s. Either way, I was happy to be free of the absolute shit-parade that Kyle called music.

~

Even at the slower speeds, we made it home in less than a day, though several energy drinks and pee breaks were necessary to do so.

We parked the Jeep along a side street in an adjacent neighborhood, and the RV in the campus parking lot using a parking pass I'd been issued earlier that year. The pass was brand new, as I'd never had a car to put it on. The weapons were safe inside the RV, seeing as nobody could get in through the side door or any of the windows. I was lucky enough to have a parking spot in full view of a security camera, which would make retrieving crates of guns difficult, but served as a wonderful deterrent for would-be thieves.

I had a pair of large duffle bags in our dorm room, which I'd originally used for moving in. We used them to transport guns, ammo, and all other manner of things that would be frowned upon on a college campus, into the room. I didn't worry too much about it, though, as we were planning to sell them to the highest bidder. We just needed them in the room long enough to take pictures of them and place the ads on the dark web. We moved everything back out into the RV when we finished, but not before Kyle picked out his gratitude payment.

He sorted through them meticulously, commenting quietly to himself as he went. He was more knowledgeable about the contents of the crates than I might have otherwise given him credit for. I guess a video game based education wasn't all bad after all.

Kyle finally settled on a mean looking rifle he called a Lapua, which was short for .338 Lapua Magnum. He claimed he could take out a deer at 1,800 yards and a moose or elk at 1,400 with the beast. As goofy as I considered Kyle to be most of the time, he looked downright scary holding his new weapon.

He tried to get me to pick something out as well, but my aversion to weapons won over and I solidly declined.

Kyle, being a better friend than I usually recognized, gave me the final say on the weapon. He informed me the gun would fetch us more than $2000 alone, and the rounds it fired were more than $5 apiece.

"I appreciate you letting me pick this out," he told me. "Are you sure? This isn't a cheap gun."

I shut that noise down quickly, telling him, "If it wasn't for you, I wouldn't have any of this. I'm sure."

Kyle genuinely looked like he was about to cry. "Thanks man," he said, showing the rare, but worthwhile, serious Kyle. "You're my best friend."

"I'm your only friend," I told him, smiling and punching him in the shoulder.

"Yeah, but there are people out there with none, or bad friends," he said. "Imagine if my best friend was a jerk. He'd still be my best friend, but a jerk. Do you know what I'm saying?"

I did, and I told him so.

~

So, remember when I said we were planning to kill someone? Yeah, I hope you didn't mind the side-story about how we got the guns, but we're finally getting back to the meat and potatoes.

As soon as we cataloged all the guns and ammo, we placed our ads. Let me be the first to tell you, the dark web is a scary place. You can find everything there, literally everything. If it's illegal, immoral, or fattening, it's there. If it's jaw-droppingly wrong, it's there. Everything from weapon sales to human trafficking occurs on the dark web. There were even offers for packaged human flesh, ready for consumption. *Consumption!* Who in the actual ballsacks goes online looking for that? Well, whoever they are, they're on there too.

In fact, it was on the dark web that we got the inspiration for our education-saving career move. Kyle and I were uploading the individual classified ads when a potential customer asked Kyle a question about the performance stats of one of the .50 caliber rifles in our inventory.

Like I said before, Kyle is like the Rain Man of guns. Hmmm, maybe that's not a good comparison. The Hugh Hefner of guns? Absolutely not. *Anyway*, he's an expert and a half.

The potential customer was practically grilling Kyle, but Kyle handled him like a n00b on an MMORPG. Kyle had all the answers and then some. Apparently, Kyle used that exact gun in the game *War is Hell* and knew its stats backward and forward.

According to Kyle, he had more than fifty confirmed kills with that weapon. Three of those kills had been at a range of almost 3,300 yards.

The buyer was duly amazed, and coyly inquired if Kyle was a trained marksman.

Well, Kyle messaged back, *with a hilariously long flight time of 7 seconds, we're getting closer to field artillery skill than marksmanship, but yes. I've been on missions all around the globe. Believe me when I say, this gun is the absolute cream of the crop.*

And those were the words that sealed the deal. Only, not in the way we'd originally planned. The buyer was so impressed, they told Kyle why they wanted the gun in the first place. There was a corrupt businessman in Las Vegas who had been cheating retirees out of their life savings in a scam that left several hundred seniors homeless, including the buyer's parents. The buyer planned to do the job themselves, but considering Kyle's skills, they wondered if he might be willing to do the job for $10,000. $5,000 up front, and the rest delivered upon confirmation of the target's demise. Before I could pull the plug on the internet, Kyle upped the arrangement to include reimbursement for the cost of travel, food, and lodging for him and his humble field operative, me.

And then it was done. Kyle turned us from would be arms dealers into contract killers.

Do you text much? Well, here's the acronym I'd use if I was texting you this story...

FML.

20
Assassins Inc.: Part 2
There are Two Asses in Assassins

Looking back on how things started, I'm amazed we didn't get arrested before we even attempted our first hit. Kyle was sure the contract was legitimate, but I was a little less certain. I kept imagining the FBI busting down our door with warrants and cheesy catchphrases. Suddenly, getting pulled over on a lonely Montana highway by a state trooper with more beer gut than sense seemed trivial.

By the next morning, however, our contact transferred a cool $5000 to the prepaid credit card Kyle used for things he didn't want his mom to know about, like MMO memberships and cases of Lightning Rod Energy Drinks. A few minutes later, an additional thousand dollars came through. Kyle checked the message board and found our 'client' sent some funds along for expenses as well. They'd followed up with a standard dossier on the subject of the hit. As if either of us actually knew what a standard dossier looked like.

Our target was an older guy named Mario Terrazzio. An additional internet search turned up more dirt on the guy than a Detroit street sweeper. He appeared to be made of Teflon, though, as no allegations of wrongdoings ever seemed to stick. Cops, prosecuting attorneys, judges, anyone who went up against the guy, either disappeared or turned up dead, but still nobody had been able to take the man down.

Until Kyle and I stepped in, that is. Teflon might protect you from egg on your face, but I was sure it wasn't bulletproof.

~

Las Vegas, the City of Lights. The city that never sleeps. The City of Sin. Did I miss anything?

No? Because I'll tell you what we did miss.

Our target.

Wait, did I skip something? Sorry, bear with me, I'll back up a bit. It'll make more sense.

We spent the week following our fortuitous online encounter with our new, revenge-seeking client, 'john_woke_1999', jockeying between class time, homework, and researching the nefarious Mario Terrazzio. Our first paid target turned out to be a pompous, arrogant creature of habit, who never went anywhere without his two bodyguards, a couple of New York-bred street brawlers named Jim and Louie. We compiled a database including everything we could find on him and his daily routines. You might be surprised by how much information a couple of starving college students can ferret out on the internet, using nothing more than public websites. Kyle has an inside track on traffic cams and other, less publicly accessible video feeds across the country, so advantage us.

Since our target was a longtime creature of habit, his daily routines, outside bilking old people out of their nest eggs, were predictable. As my favorite superhero, the Golden Sentinel, once said, "arrogance breeds complacency." And this chump appeared as complacent as a union worker on a long lunch break.

Using the money on Kyle's credit card, we booked a Friday afternoon flight to Las Vegas. We disassembled the .50 cal and packed it and the ammo accordingly. By Friday evening, we were looking over the Las Vegas skyline from our 14th floor hotel window. Kyle insisted on reminding me that since hotels never included the 13th floor on their listings, we were technically on the 'real' 13th floor. He bought into all sorts of superstitions, things about ladders, broken mirrors, rabbit's feet, you name it. He was cool with black cats, though. Hey, I'll admit it, I don't understand him any more than you do.

We spent that evening in the casino, enjoying free drinks and losing at blackjack. Even Kyle's lucky rabbit's foot couldn't improve our odds. The next morning, we took a cab out towards the dog track. Aside from being a functioning alcoholic and smoking more cigars than Cuba could produce in a year, Terrazzio's most predictable vice was betting on the Greyhound races. For the record, I thought dog racing was cruel and gross, making him an even more appropriate target for a hit.

He always bet on the first three races of the day, then took his limo to a private country club, where he'd drink and hit balls into a net until dark. Our best shot was getting him from a ridge on a hilltop near the racetrack. According to Kyle, getting him coming in would be difficult, as to set up a shot, he'd need more than a few seconds to dial him in and compensate for wind. We had one shot, literally, to take out Terrazzio and earn our $10,000. By the way, I hate people who use the word literally incorrectly almost as much as I hate people who bet on dog races and take advantage of old people.

Once we were in position in a tall patch of weeds that obscured us from view of the track, and most everything else, Kyle unzipped the duffle bag and removed the beast.

A moment after Kyle laid the gun's parts out onto a couple of borrowed hotel bath towels, we observed Terrazzio's limo entering the gated parking lot. Seconds later, it vanished into the already impressive mass of limousines and cars inside.

Kyle assembled the .50 cal a little more slowly than I'd expected, considering his tales of war glories.

"Are you sure in-game experience prepared you properly for real-world shooting," I asked, more than a bit concerned. I was never really a gamer, so I guess I'd just taken Kyle at his word.

"It's exactly the same, bruh," he replied, fumbling with the barrel assembly. "I'm a crack shot on this rig."

"Okay." I shrugged. "I hope so." I was beginning to wonder if 'john_woke_1999' was going to be asking for their money back come Monday.

Once he finally assembled the gun, Kyle popped a short magazine into the stock, unfolded the bi-pod, and set it carefully on the ground in front of us. He then began fiddling with the gun sight, turning knobs, and cursing softly as he peered through it.

I reached forward and popped the dust cap off the front of the sight. "Better," I asked, feeling less confident by the second.

Kyle grunted softly and clicked the safety to make sure it was properly engaged. "We're good," he lied. "Now we just wait. When the mark leaves the lot, I should have about 15 seconds to sight a shot and take him out."

"How did you calculate the 15-second window," I asked, not feeling too confident in his estimate.

"I've been watching other cars leave and timing them," he said. He rolled out a bedsheet in the grass and laid on his stomach. "I've got this," he said, adjusting the sight again.

His answer restored a bit my faith in him. I laid down next to him and focused on the parking lot gates.

~

A little over an hour later, Terrazzio's black Lincoln Town Car pulled up to the parking lot exit and turned left onto the access road.

Kyle was in motion before I realized he was reacting, and I kept my mouth shut. I refused to be the only reason Kyle's shot missed.

Turns out it didn't help.

As the limo moved lazily along the access road, giving Kyle more time than he'd even calculated, my best friend in the world, whispered, "Do you feel lucky, punk," and fired.

We both watched with bated breath as the projectile made its way towards our target's car. Now I know I told you he missed Terrazzio already. What I didn't tell you, is what he did hit.

~

The bullet couldn't have been further off. It was like Kyle was shooting at elk, if elk lived in the clouds. My friend was more crackpot than crack shot.

Initially, it was hard to see where the bullet was headed, as Kyle chose armor piercing rounds instead of tracers. But when it struck the power line twenty feet ahead of the limo, that bullet was the impetus of the world's deadliest, and possibly most profitable Rube Goldberg machine. Alright, so OK Go might have us on the profitable end, but we take the prize for deadly for sure.

The power line dropped like a snake from a tree, landing on a roadside propane tank, and spitting sparks like an angry electric cat! Almost immediately, the massive fuel tank exploded with such ferocity, we could feel a wave of heat wash over our hiding place. Shrapnel flew in all directions, including into the limo. I'm sure it got the driver because the vehicle swerved out of control, finally slamming into a tree next to the still burning tank. Surprisingly, Terrazzio was still alive. We knew that because a second or two later, the back door of the limo opened, and the rotund reprobate wobbled out of the car, shaken, but very much alive.

Kyle chambered another round and lined up a shot, though after seeing his first one, I was sure we were screwed. But before Kyle could pull the trigger, a second explosion erupted from the tank, engulfing the limo in a hellish torrent of white flames. When the fire receded, Terrazzio was gone.

~

We walked a few miles before hopping onto a city bus, taking public transportation back to our hotel. During the longest 35-minute ride of our lives, a teenage boy looked at Kyle's duffle bag, which reeked of gun oil, and asked, "Whatcha' got in the bag? It smells bad."

Without even looking up, Kyle replied, "baseball gear. You probably smell the glove oil."

The kid looked satisfied with the answer. "Nice, man. Batting cages?"

Kyle nodded somberly.

"Any good hits," the kid asked.

"Kid," Kyle groaned, "you have no idea."

~

We skipped our flight home, opting to not tempt fate with airport security. Instead, we took the bus. It took nearly thirteen hours by road as opposed to two by air, but we both needed some time to quietly decompress. We barely said a word to each other the entire trip.

Monday came around, as Mondays always do. As we were watching a news report about a freak fatality accident on the outskirts of Las Vegas, Kyle's laptop dinged, telling him he had a message.

He had several messages, actually. One thanking us for the brilliant, quality service we provided, and another telling us the remaining $5,000 had been deposited, plus an extra $2,000 for 'making it look like an accident'.

The rest of the messages were from other users asking about our services. We were quite a hit.

Pun intended.

21
Back to Life, Back to Surreality

When I woke up, I was still in the leather office chair, in the same position I'd fallen asleep in. The dreams of random games came almost nightly, as if I was accessing a giant file cabinet, reading files one by one, trying to piece together the world's biggest unsolved mystery. The RV from *Assassins Inc.* popped back into my head. All those file boxes were like my memories, waiting to be opened and pored over. Instead of being easier to separate reality from fiction, it was getting more difficult.

Becky's presence blurred the line even more.

How could I possibly focus on what was real, when someone I knew to be fictional was living and breathing just down the hall? I wondered, as did every day, if I was still in a medically induced coma somewhere, spiraling deeper and deeper into the delusion that seemed to be consuming my life.

If that was the case, then my psychosis was on an *Inception* level, and the layers would probably never stop peeling away. I chose to believe in the weirdness my world had become. As unsettling as my current situation was, the idea that my broken subconscious was dragging me down like a struggling quicksand victim was downright terrifying.

I suddenly wished to be back asleep, in a place where my reality wasn't in question, and all my thoughts made sense, no matter how ludicrous they might seem to others.

I was happy to see Becky. I can't lie and say I wasn't. But her presence tossed everything I thought I knew about myself and the world around me right out the window. I was grateful for dad and Irene's help and support, especially Irene's at that moment, since dad seemed more floored than me.

I had to keep in mind though, as difficult as this was to grasp for any of us, it had to be even harder for Becky. She was the stranger in a strange land, not me.

I looked around and found that dad had left the room sometime during my nap.

I poked my head into the hall and heard voices coming from the nanoperating room. Dad's was clearly one of them. I decided to join them, hoping Irene might finally have some answers.

~

Irene had answers, but I'm not sure they made me feel any better. They certainly didn't seem to ease Becky's mind.

"Becky is as real as any of us, Packard," she told me when I asked about the verdict. "However, as much as I can say she's real, and that I believe she's sentient, and even that she's flesh and blood, there's more to her than meets the eye."

Becky shifted uncomfortably in the big chair. I knew all too well how it felt being the one sitting there, getting talked about, instead of talked to.

"Are you okay," I asked her. "Can I get you anything? Water? A snack?"

She shook her head. "No, I'm not hungry, and I have a water already." She held up her hand, which was white knuckling a plastic water bottle. It crackled in her hand as she squeezed. "But thank you anyway."

"Of course," I replied, before turning back to Irene. "So, what else do we know?"

Irene pulled up a chart on one of her wall-mounted screens. The data meant nothing to me, but I was sure she would explain. I looked at Gunner, who stood next to dad squeezing a grip strengthener. Becky sure could have used one of those. Gunner shrugged, clearly as much in the dark as I was. Dad looked interested, but still scarily concerned.

"I've taken a series of blood samples from Becky over the past few hours. On the surface they appear normal, but a closer inspection proves otherwise." She pointed at a series of columns on the chart. "Most techs would never think to look for Nanops in a person's bloodstream. Most facilities wouldn't have equipment capable of detecting them. Just the CDC and a few other places geared towards looking for anomalies, as opposed to run-of-the-mill drugs, contaminates, or toxins." She took a swig of water before returning her focus to the screen. "Like I said, Becky, on the surface, your blood work appears normal. What's *not* normal are the Nanops in your bloodstream and the fact that with every subsequent blood draw, their levels are decreasing."

Dad cleared his throat. "And the DNA? You mentioned there was something of interest in her DNA as well, correct?"

I was no scientist, but hearing that Becky had DNA was a convincing argument for her being the genuine article.

Irene nodded. "Yes. I'll put it into the simplest terms I'm able. Human DNA is 99.9% identical from person to person. Although a 0.1% difference doesn't sound like a lot, it represents millions of different locations within the genome where variations can occur, equating to a breathtakingly large number of potentially unique DNA sequences." She looked between Becky and me. "You two share an almost identical upper 0.1%. That's unheard of outside same-sex identical twins, which you're clearly not."

"What are you saying," Becky asked. "That Packard and I are related? Like he's my brother or something?"

At least she didn't say dad, I thought.

"Or her dad," Gunner piped in.

Thanks, Gunner. Thanks for destroying my life.

Irene shook her head. "You could interpret it that way, but no. That would be like Hal jumping my car battery with his car and saying his car was powering mine after removing the jumper cables." She pulled up another visual that looked like it came from a heart monitor. "Becky, I was able to read your DNA sequence from an oscilloscope. While it's clear Packard's DNA was a template, yours is mutating as fast as the Nanops are vanishing from your blood. That 0.1% is changing, meaning you're evolving."

"Into what," Becky asked, looking sick and scared.

Irene smiled gently. "Into *you*, I think. Your DNA is adapting to who you're supposed to be."

~

I think Becky felt better after Irene's explanation. She asked for another water, and when I offered her a snack again, she accepted an apple and some peanut butter.

"I have a question for you," she said quietly as we walked back down the hall to the meeting room. Her voice still betrayed the worry she was obviously dog paddling around in.

"Anything," I said, hoping she wouldn't bring up the brother or dad thing again.

"Before I appeared here, the last thing I remember was something really awful and scary." She took a deep breath. Something was really eating at her. "I saw you die, Pack. We were on that field trip and the monsters attacked. Mr. Pan, Stan, they died right before you. But you were the worst because you screamed the longest." She shivered, even though the room wasn't cold. "And then I was here. Nobody could see me, and you wouldn't answer me. I tried to be strong, but there were times I just wanted to lay down and scream."

I didn't know what to say. My mind flashed back to the memories from the game. As bad as that experience was for me, it was somehow her reality. She had to watch so many of us die. "I'm sorry," I whispered. "I didn't mean to-" I stopped. There was nothing I could say that would make any of what she was feeling better.

"One minute, I was standing next to Brad, and the next... how are we here," she asked, her eyes wrestling with her emotions and a barrage of conflicting thoughts. "Do you know these people? This seems like your life or something, but I know you, don't I? This isn't your life, is it?" She sighed, but it was one of those sighs that precedes tears, like a thunderclap before a downpour. "I've been trying to accept everything, but what's going on? Am I really here? Are you? Am I even *real?*"

I took her in my arms and hugged her for all I was worth, feeling about as lost as the 'g' in lasagna. "I've been wondering the same thing about myself, Beck, but I think we both know the answer. We're both real, and we're both here. This isn't some fever dream or neural intelligence interface. As twisted as it all feels, this is reality. I'm here with you right now, and I'm not going anywhere."

Becky looked at me for a moment, her eyes welling up with tears. She nodded weakly. "Thank you, Pack." Then the tears she'd been holding off so bravely finally came.

~

The adults wisely remained scarce while Becky sobbed, sometimes violently, into my chest. Becky had experienced a form of trauma most psychologists would scratch their heads over. She'd seen and heard things nobody should ever have to. She had even bravely come through what she thought was being a ghost and smiled like nothing had happened when I'd finally acknowledged her. I'd failed her, but never again.

After Becky cried every tear her poor body could produce, dad, Irene, and Gunner entered the meeting room and closed the door behind them. There were other Arete employees leaving for the day through that corridor, and they had no business hearing our conversation.

The five of us spent the next hour talking. Actually, dad, Irene, Becky, and I talked, while Gunner stood menacingly, massive arms crossed, just inside the door, and listened.

Becky asked hundreds of questions, while dad, Irene, and I filled in as many blanks as possible. It was quite possibly the most awkward game of twenty questions ever.

Explaining to Becky that, to us, she was a fictional character my dad created to move a video game's story along, was like telling a piglet he was born to be bacon. It was like a violation of her spirit. It took some time for her to grasp the fact that, while the version of me in the game wasn't actually me, in a roundabout way, the person she got to know was me. There was even a full minute where she sat quietly and just glared at dad.

"Are all the bad things that ever happened to me your fault," she asked, scowling. Her expression wasn't exactly hatred, but I think I finally understood what contempt looked like.

Dad was pale. I knew him, his heart, his empathy. He was hurting as much as Becky was. He sighed, that thunderclap preceding tears present in his voice as well. "Honestly, Becky, I don't know." He couldn't look her in the eye. Even though there wasn't anything he could have done differently, he was ashamed. "I was writing games, creating entertainment. I couldn't have known that somewhere in the universe, you might be-" He sighed again, so deeply I thought he might pass out. "You might be real."

Irene cleared her throat, drawing the attention, and Becky's ire, onto herself. "It's clear the Nanops are somehow responsible for you being here. Therefore, as hard as it is to say, whether directly or indirectly, I'm as liable for your appearance as Hal is."

Becky pursed her lips. She wanted to be mad, but she obviously wasn't that guy. She knew neither of them had done anything to intentionally bring her into our world. They'd been doing work that benefitted society. When tragedy struck, they used their work to try to save a life, *my* life. There was no way they could have even dreamed up the insane scenario we were all suddenly faced with.

Becky shook her head. "It's just so darned crazy." She stood and walked to the window, looking out over the Arete campus. The afternoon sun filtered through wisps of clouds and 100+ year old oak trees lining the park-like setting outside. She put her fingertips against the glass. Maybe she was feeling the warmth of the sun on the pane, maybe trying to connect with something outside, maybe she was just wishing she was somewhere else, anywhere else. "The day of the field trip was just like this one." She turned. Her eyes softened, and the accusing scowl vanished. "It was perfect, and then it wasn't."

"We're going to try to figure out how to get you home, Becky," Irene offered.

Dad nodded, finally making eye contact with her.

"Is my home even real," Becky wondered aloud.

I raised my hand. Hey, I'm polite. I don't like to interrupt. "I think you're real, and wherever you came from is real, too," I said. "You didn't just come from my memories. You knew things I didn't. And you... you just have to be real."

Becky didn't smile at that, but she didn't frown either. She was hurting and trying to process.

"Thank you," she said to all of us.

Gunner looked up at her.

"Yeah, you too," she smiled finally.

"Well, boo hoo," a familiar voice said behind me.

Becky's eyes widened as Gunner rapidly drew his sidearm, leveling it at something, or someone I couldn't see. His face suddenly became the terrifying reason I imagined Irene had hired him in the first place.

"Drop it," Gunner commanded. "Drop it NOW!"

I practically fell out of my chair and dropped to the floor between Gunner and our unexpected visitor. I turned while scooting under the large, hardwood table. And then I stopped, putting my hand up again. "It's okay, Gunner," I shouted. "I know this guy."

I stood slowly and deliberately, putting myself between Gunner and the tall, lanky man with the cowboy hat and polished silver revolver. "Howdy, Clem." I was smiling, but I suddenly felt like my stomach was using my colon as a hula-hoop.

22

Meanwhile, Back at the Ranch

If Becky threw my understanding of everything out the window, then Clem Pickett came crashing through it like a drunk in a bar fight.

The lost lawman looked at me curiously for a moment, before lowering his weapon slightly. "Marshal," he said, sounding as confused as everyone in the room felt. "Why're you dressed that way, Marshal," he asked suspiciously. "And where are your sidearms?"

I put my other hand in the air, hoping to signal a truce. "I'll explain as soon as you re-holster that cold lead-slinger. Alright, Clem?"

Clem leered at Gunner. Unfortunately, I knew exactly what was going through his head.

"Gunner," I said, "whatever he says, don't let him get to you. Please put down the gun, and I'll get him to do the same, okay? Please trust me on this. He's like Becky, from somewhere else, please."

Clem snorted. "I'll re-holster Jackson after your dark-skinned friend here re-holsters his strange-lookin' hand-cannon."

And there it was.

The only thing worse than Clem. *His mouth.* Or maybe it was his opinions, since he always voiced them. Aw, hell, Clem was just awful all the way around.

Gunner's grasp tightened audibly around his pistol grip. He was furious and had every right to be. But Clem was being, well, the bigoted, xenophobic, homophobic, racist, sexist, piece of crap who had so selflessly saved my skin in more than one play through of *Marshal Blood.*

"What. Did. You. Just. Say," Gunner growled.

Clem sneered. "You heard me, ni-"

"WOAH!" I hollered, drowning out the rest of Clem's word. Dad, Irene, and Becky wisely hit the floor, but there I was, standing between two gun-toting adversaries like the world's worst negotiator. "Please! Nobody needs to get hurt! I really don't want to die here, guys, so *please!* You're both lawmen, *now act like it!*"

Not surprisingly, Gunner was the first to extend the olive branch, lowering his .45 to a position just above his holster, but still ready to aim from the hip if Clem forced his hand. "Okay, friend," he said begrudgingly. "Let's do this together, shall we?"

For another tense moment, Clem's eyes remained narrowed, like he was mocking Clint Eastwood. Then, following Gunner's lead, he gently thumbed the hammer on his six-shooter into a safe position. After another moment's hesitation, he holstered it, matching Gunner's movements with the precision of a seasoned, deadly gunfighter.

I let my breath exit my chest in a loud whoosh, feeling my heart hammering in my chest, and my feet begin to thaw. "Thank you," I sighed. "Thank you both."

"Not many colored lawmen in these here parts," Clem started.

"Oh, please, Clem," I shouted. "Will you just stop?!"

Clem looked like I'd struck him. "Apologies, Marshal. I wuz jest statin' a fact."

"First of all, Clem, those aren't facts anymore. Secondly, the apology shouldn't be to me." I motioned towards Gunner. "If anyone deserves an apology, it's Gunner. I don't want any excuses or explanations, just an old-fashioned apology. Can you do that?"

Clem tipped his hat slightly at Gunner. "Sincerest apologies, lawman," he said. "The name's Clem Pickett, duly elected sheriff of Rotgut, Arizona. And who might you be?"

Gunner was still unsure of the madness taking place in the Arete building, or how he fit into any of it. But he did recognize the Herculean effort it took cantankerous ol' Clem to apologize. "I'm Gunner," he replied calmly, adding a bit more bass to his voice than usual. "Gunner Reeves. Chief of Security here at Arete Nanophysiology."

Clem's eyes widened. "Reeves?" He tossed the name around in his head for a moment. "Might you be a relation of the legendary Bass Reeves," he asked, suddenly seeming a bit starstruck.

Gunner nodded. "He was my great, great, uh, some level of grandfather several generations back." Gunner visibly relaxed as he spoke. "His story inspired me to get into law enforcement, but a crooked spine kept me from going all the way with it, so here I am. Security."

"A lawman's a lawman," Clem said with more reverence than I'd ever heard in the old codger's raspy voice. "Protectin' folk's a noble callin', white, black, yeller, don't matter. Any kin of Bass Reeves, distant or t'other, is right fine by me. Pleased to make your acquaintance."

I was shocked. Could it be that ol' Clem had more to him than I'd ever seen in the games?

He turned back to me and extended a leathery, calloused hand. "Presently, I'm about as confused as a blind priest in a cathouse, but it's nice to see you, Marshal." We shook hands and he nodded towards Becky, who was getting to her feet with dad and Irene. "I ain't too clear on what you meant when you said this lil' filly and me are the same, but I'll chalk it up to crazy talk on account of tensions between me and ol' Black Gunner Reeves, here."

Becky bristled, and a collective sigh filled the room as Gunner snapped his holster shut, clearly avoiding any temptation to just end Clem and his nonsense on the spot.

I patted Clem on a narrow, bony shoulder. "We don't identify people by their race, color, gender, or *anything* like that anymore, Clem."

"Lady Gaga," Dad mumbled.

"Not helping dad," I said, before continuing. "Clem, my friend, we've got a lot to talk about if you're going to get along in this world."

~

While receptive on the surface to the clearly outlandish concepts we shared regarding racial and gender equality, sexual freedoms, and a litany of other social faux pas he could commit between the boardroom and the bathroom, Clem was going to be nearly impossible to take anywhere public.

He was dismissive of Becky and Irene based on their gender. And of course, Irene, being of Asian descent, had two strikes on the Clem-o-meter. If Gunner hadn't had the last name

Reeves, he would've been as low or lower on Clem's backwards scale of human judgement. I can't honestly say how I'd ever trusted my life to a man who valued his horse's judgement over a woman's, but in the heat of battle loyalty means something, I suppose.

Becky and Irene were both livid by that point. I found myself grateful neither of them had a gun of their own.

Gunner leaned in towards dad. "So, you uh… wrote this character, huh?" His voice still carried more than the usual amount of bass.

Dad squirmed in his seat. "I was going for historical accuracy," he croaked sheepishly.

Gunner straightened up. "I see. This coming from a guy who thought it was appropriate to create a game where college students smuggle firearms into their dorm room, eh?"

Irene shook her head at Gunner, indicating he was going too far. Gunner wisely backed off and joined the united front against Clem's nonsense.

Clem still didn't understand how an Asian woman could be educated, let alone have two doctorates in scientific fields. "It's just unheard of," Clem insisted. "It is, and always will be, a man's world," he declared.

Gunner leaned towards Irene. "I could still shoot him."

This prompted Clem to stand and place his hand on the butt of his gun.

"Just kidding," Gunner sighed. "We're on the same team here, pard. I promise."

Clem looked at me, clearly seeking reassurance. "You can trust him with your life," I said.

Gunner nodded.

"And the fillies," Clem asked, eliciting the deadliest looks out of Irene and Becky.

"Jesus, Clem," I said, losing patience. "You're going to have to trust me on this. They're your equal. Honestly, I'm pretty certain *no one* is *Irene's* equal."

Then, as if the day hadn't been bad enough, an alarm sounded on dad's phone.

"It's the security system," dad said, sounding worried. "We have a break-in."

He pulled up his security feed on his phone and gasped. Standing in the middle of our kitchen, eating apples from the bowl on the center island, was my horse.

"Whisper," Clem said, looking over dad's shoulder.

Just then, dad's phone rang.

"Shhh," he said. "It's the security company." He answered his phone as calmly as a man who just realized a fictional horse was standing in the middle of his kitchen could. "This is Hal Campbell. Yes, I'm aware of the alarm. No, no need to pull the footage! I'm sorry? No, everything is fine. It's our dog, Whisper." Dad laughed at something the operator said. "Yes, she's new to the household. I'll be sure to reset the sensors. Oh, the code? 22106." He grimaced as the person continued. "Yes, I understand. No, you're right, we certainly don't want to get fined for false alarms. I'll fix it. Yes. Thank you." Dad hung up and looked from Irene to me, and then the others. "Apparently there's a horse in my kitchen. We need to go home before the security company pulls the video feed. I'm sure there's a city ordinance prohibiting citizens from keeping horses in their home."

Irene put her hands up in the 'what else could go wrong' gesture. "It goes against my better judgement to let you take Becky and Clem with you."

Becky was at her wit's end. "Am I a prisoner here?"

That sent Clem's hand directly to his pistol. "I ain't nobody's prizzner," he declared loudly.

"Nobody is a prisoner here," Irene assured them both. "There's just still so much I need to know." She looked at dad, trying to decide what to say next. "Are you okay taking them with you?"

Dad nodded. "I'm sure everyone needs a cool-down period. What do you say we continue this discussion on Monday?"

Irene reluctantly agreed.

So, after introducing Clem to the indoor outhouse, *and showing him how to wash his hands*, he fervently shook the hand of the kin of one of his childhood idols. Then Becky hugged Irene and Gunner, and the four of us headed out into the real world, together.

23

Between Whisper and a Dream

As we stepped out through Arete's huge front doors, Becky caught her breath. She put out her fingers again, this time feeling the breeze play across them, and she smiled as the last heated spears of the day's sunlight pricked at her fingertips. Her light brown, shoulder-length hair swayed as a late summer breeze greeted us.

Dad and I watched as she and Clem took in the view. They both seemed awestruck. As anxious as I knew dad was to get home and find out what kind of mayhem Whisper was causing in our house, he gently clasped my shoulder, stopping me a few feet behind them. I have to admit, it was pure magic, watching each of them taking in the beauty of the tree-lined campus and the rolling hills of grass. Becky breathed in deeply, put her head back, and finally turned, her eyes meeting mine. A glimmer of hope absent earlier shone there, and my heart felt better than it had in weeks, maybe ever.

"I can feel it," Becky declared, her excited smile breaking thorough the gloom.

"Feel what," I asked, obviously taking something for granted.

"Reality," she said, almost whispering it. She was trying not to cry. "I was so afraid I was dead, or maybe I wasn't real, but this feeling..." She trailed off, knowing if she said anything else, she'd lose her battle with some intense emotions.

Clem, of course, had to ruin it by opening his mouth. "The air smells funny here, Marshal." He looked around the campus, always the lawman, eyes narrowed, suspiciously taking in every detail. I often forgot, considering how narrow his views were, what an adept sheriff he was. "I've been to New York City, but them buildins' on yonder horizon ain't like nothin' I ever seen." He looked at my dad and me, wrinkling his face a bit. "Y'ain't never steered me wrong, ol' friend. So I'm fixin' to trust you. I jest need to know where the hell we are."

I nodded. Even though he ignored Becky's statement, he had a valid concern. "Clem, my dad, uh, Pa and I will explain everything while we're on the road. I need you to remember you're not the only one here. You interrupted Becky."

Becky shook her head. "Thanks, Pack, but I was done talking."

"See, Marshal," Clem gloated. "I did no such thang."

I wasn't going to stand there arguing with a man who could win a staring contest with Medusa, so I agreed and moved on. I pointed to dad's Subaru. "Hop in, then. Let's hit the road."

Clem looked at dad's car, the mask of suspicion still firmly in place. "Y'ain't even hitched any horses up to your funny lookin' wagon." He glanced at the sun, which was just beginning to drop behind the foothills to the west. "It's gonna' be slow goin' once it gets dark. Mayhaps we should jest pitch camp here, and travel in the mornin'?"

I sighed. Clem would learn eventually, but he was going to be a tough, and likely resistant student. Thankfully, he wasn't a Puritan or something. The car, the phone, everything would probably feel like witchcraft to someone like that. To Clem, though, it was still going to be one hell of a learning curve.

As Becky and I followed dad to the car, a roar echoed overhead. Clem dropped to one knee like a weird, Old West Spider-Man, and began firing his revolver into the sky.

I broke away from Becky and dove through the air, tackling Clem, and knocking the gun from his hand.

"What the hell," I asked loudly.

"Strangest damned bird I ever seen," Clem exclaimed.

"What the HELL!?" A voice loudly repeated my sentiment from across the grass.

I looked up to see Gunner running towards us, his .45 drawn once again, but thankfully pointed at the ground.

"It's okay," I shouted back. "Clem just saw his first airplane."

~

It took more than a few minutes to convince Clem to stow his sidearm in the back of dad's car, and another few minutes to get him inside the 'queer looking contraption' himself.

At Gunner's suggestion, I wrapped the sidearm in one of our beach towels and placed the bundle inside dad's ice chest. The big man wanted to wrap the chest in duct tape, just in case, but I suggested Clem just ride up front with dad. We wanted him far away from his pistol. If I thought we could get away with leaving it with Gunner, I would have, but I also understood the wisdom of picking one's battles wisely.

Before getting in and finally fastening his seatbelt – it took dad demonstrating the action with his belt three times first – Clem studied dad's car closely. "So, you say it's a horseless carriage," he commented, kicking the tires. "The wheels seem flimsy. Perhaps wood would be sturdier? It looks to me like a steam engine copulated with some manner of stagecoach. Do ya' need me to ride up top with my gun, Marshal's Pa?"

"Good lord," dad replied. "Just get in."

I won't lie, I wasn't sad to be sitting in the back with Becky. Either of the other options weren't great, but Becky sitting in the back alone with Clem was just a recipe for disaster. I know I don't give him nearly enough credit, but I've known him for a long time. Given enough leeway, he'd just piss her off.

Clem held onto dad's favorite 'oh, shit handle' for the first few minutes of the drive, but by the time we hit the freeway a few minutes later, he appeared to be enjoying the ride. Dad took the opportunity to explain some things Clem had seen and would likely be seeing in the near future. He started with the airplane, which Clem found to be 'downright unbelievable' if he hadn't seen it with his own eyes. Dad then moved onto motorized land vehicles, which he explained mostly all operated under similar principles, but varied in size and number of wheels. A brief rundown of a cellphone, personal computer, refrigerator, flashlight, and a few other novelties followed, and before we knew it, we were pulling into our garage in good ol' Noe Valley.

Becky fell asleep on my shoulder the moment we hit the freeway. Tell me she could have done that sitting with Clem. Okay, so she was exhausted since she didn't have the benefit of a nap like dad and me. Maybe she still would've dozed off, but I'm sure I was more comfortable, and I know I smelled better.

"And we're home," Dad announced, hurrying to get inside the house to see if Whisper was horsing around. Funny? Not funny? I don't hear you laughing. Anyway, dad stopped just shy of the garage door and turned to me. "Maybe you should go in first, seeing as she's your horse?"

I pulled away from Becky, leaving her snoring gently in the back seat while Clem struggled with his seatbelt. "Just push the red button, Clem," I said before hopping out of the car. "Dad, it's Whisper," I smiled.

He raised a bushy eyebrow. "That may be, son, but she still knows you, not me."

I jogged up to the door, and patted dad on the shoulder as I went into the house. "Clem needs your help. And Becky fell asleep."

~

Now, when I say Whisper is the best horse ever, I mean that with every fiber of my being. She's the quintessential horse. Loyal like a dog, smart like a cat, agile like a, um, cat, but still 100% horse. If you told me she was even remotely capable of destroying the inside of our house, I would have told you that you were dead wrong.

And I would have been right.

When I walked into the kitchen, aside from the apple bowl being empty, the house was just as we'd left it. As soon as Whisper saw me, she pranced around like a show horse.

"Whisper!" I skipped over to my trusty fictitious steed and hugged her tightly. She continued to prance nervously until I realized what she was doing. "Oh my gosh," I exclaimed. "You need to go potty, don't you!?"

Whisper whinnied excitedly, continuing what I now realized was the pee-pee dance. I bolted to the back door and opened it. She trotted out the door. A moment later, I could hear her relieving herself on the back lawn. I stepped out onto the patio, still hardly believing the turn our day had taken, and was continuing to take.

From the patio, I could hear the others coming in through the garage. Clem was complaining to dad about his gun, saying he needed it, and felt naked without it. "You wouldn't want me naked now, would you, Marshal's Pa," Clem asked loudly.

An uncomfortable silence followed, finally broken by one of dad's more exasperated sighs. "No," he agreed emphatically. "But I don't need you shooting anymore airplanes. Gunner had to lie to the cops after your public weapons discharge."

"He lied?" Clem sounded surprised. "That goes against the Lawman's Code."

Dad rolled his eyes. He looked tired. "Clem, what would you tell them? A cowboy who shouldn't exist in our world shot at an airplane because he mistook it for a bird?"

Clem cleared his throat, sounding a bit embarrassed. "Well, when you put it that way, I do suppose it sounds right preposterous, don't it?"

"Yes, Clem. It does," dad agreed.

"Well then," Clem continued thoughtfully, "please tell Lawman Reeves I'm genuinely sorry for putting him in that there position. No lawman should have to lie."

As dad and Clem continued their discussion, Becky stepped out onto the patio and joined me in watching Whisper. "So, we're watching your horse pee," she asked, feigning interest.

"Uh, I-" Anything I could say in response would've sounded stupid.

"Hal Campbell is that you," a voice called out. It was old Mrs. Bumblesnaps, our next door neighbor. "Hello Hal, and my, don't you look lovely tonight, Victoria."

"Oh, hi, Mrs. Bumblesnaps," I replied. "I'm not-"

"Dear me, Hal, is that a horse!?" Our neighbor squinted in the moonlight, adjusting her glasses.

She caught us. "Oh, uh, no. It's uh-"

"Hello, Mrs. Bumblesnaps," Becky chimed in. "It's so nice to see you again." Becky cringed at me, and feeling a bit trapped, I cringed back. "You're such a kidder, aren't you," she continued. "This is our new dog, Whisper."

Whisper and Mrs. Bumblesnaps both turned to look at Becky. Whisper grunted disapprovingly.

"Your dog?" Our neighbor was half-blind, and a little senile, but even she wouldn't fall for that one.

"She's a Great Dane," Becky said, matter-of-factly. "Pure bred."

"Oh," Mrs. Bumblesnaps laughed, still clearly confused. "What a beautiful dog she is, and so big."

Whisper whinnied defiantly before trotting into the house.

"Good girl," Becky exclaimed. "Good night, Mrs. Bumblesnaps! Nice seeing you!"

I waved to our neighbor as I followed Becky back into the house, closing the door behind us.

Clem stood by the refrigerator, a beer in one hand, and a snow globe from New York in the other. "This don't look anything like the New York I remember," he said, already a bit tipsy.

"Most of the buildings in there would have been built long after you would've been there," I replied as Becky patted Whisper's neck.

"Good girl," Becky crooned before turning to me. "Who's Victoria," she asked casually.

"Victoria was my mom," I said quietly. "Mrs. Bumblesnaps knew them when they were kids, too." Before Becky could ask anything else, I turned to Clem. "Where's my pa?"

"Out yonder," he said, pointing at the garage with the bottleneck. "I reckon he's retrievin' my lead-slinger."

I left Becky petting Whisper, and Clem nursing on his beer, and went outside to find dad.

Dad was standing, empty-handed, next to my Pontiac.

"You okay, dad," I asked.

"Come here," he said, clearly distracted. "Tell me what you see."

I walked over to Knightmare and peered in. The top was already down, so we had an unobstructed view of the interior.

"Anything seem off," Dad asked.

I shook my head for a moment before it hit me. Then I couldn't unsee it. "Are those buttons new," I asked.

Dad nodded grimly. "Yeah, and only half of them were there when I first came back out. The rest grew over the last couple of minutes."

"Grew?" I must have sounded like I didn't believe him.

"Becky, Clem, Whisper," dad started. "Can you honestly tell me anything surprises you today," he asked.

I was about to answer him when a calm, almost alien voice greeted us from within the car. "Hello, Packard."

"Kni- Knightmare," I stammered.

"Were you expecting the Batmobile, perhaps," Knightmare replied. Yup, it was her.

I looked at dad. I could tell he wanted to think our new talking car was cool. The seventeen-year-old kid in him was probably pumping his fist in the air, saying, 'Holy crap, a talking car!' But the man standing next to me wasn't seventeen anymore, and he looked scared as hell.

"Packard, go inside," Dad said.

His voice chilled my blood. He was at his breaking point. "Dad," I began to say.

"Go back in the *HOUSE*," dad shouted. "Now, son!"

I wanted so badly to be willful and anti-authoritarian. But I also knew if I chose that moment to assert my manhood, my relationship with dad would fundamentally change forever.

I wasn't ready for that.

"Okay," I said with as much respect as I could muster.

As the kitchen door closed behind me, I glanced back and saw dad climb into the driver's seat. A moment later, Knightmare started, and dad drove away.

24
Epilogue

About an hour had passed since dad and Knightmare drove off, and honestly, I was worried sick.

Clem fell asleep on the couch after only one beer and Whisper stood in the dark by our kitchen window, looking out at our neighbor's apple trees longingly.

Becky sat next to me on the loveseat. She watched me silently, probably knowing I was trying to process too much at once.

I couldn't take it anymore. I had to do something, but I felt helpless. Looking at Clem, I realized his boots were still on and propped up on dad's favorite throw pillows. I picked Clem's hat up off the floor and handed it to Becky, nodding at the row of pegs by the front door. She walked over and hung it on one of the empty ones. When she turned, I was removing Clem's boots.

"Are you sure you want to," Becky started to ask as the first boot slipped free. "Christ almighty," she exclaimed. "Put it back on!"

I gagged as I pried the other boot off and ran the pair to the back door. Whisper offered a judgmental grunt when she caught a whiff of the bad boys on their way out. "You think those are bad, you should smell his socks," I replied, still gagging.

Becky wisely retrieved a can of air freshener from the guest bathroom and sprayed it directly onto his feet. "Sorry, I wasn't brave enough to remove his socks," she apologized.

I grabbed a blanket from the hall closet and draped it over Clem's feet, immediately making the room habitable again.

Clem rolled a bit and mumbled something about smelling pretty flowers, then he resumed his snoring.

"Crisis averted!" Becky put up a hand for a high five, but I missed the gesture for a moment. When I finally recognized her intention, I returned the five, but less enthusiastically than she hoped for.

"You wanna talk," she asked.

"Not really," I began. "I just need to-" My phone rang. The number wasn't in my contacts, but I answered it anyway, hoping. "Dad," I said nervously.

"No, Packard. It's Gunner, man."

It's Gunner, I mouthed to Becky.

"Hey, Gunner. My dad's not here," I started to say.

"It was you I needed," Gunner replied. "Can you come back to Arete?" He sounded less calm and Gunner-like than I was comfortable with.

"Now," I asked. "It's like ten p.m., and my dad's not here. I don't have a license."

"Crap, okay." Gunner was clearly having a difficult time with something.

"Gunner, are you okay," I asked. "What's going on? Is Irene okay?"

Gunner didn't speak for a moment, then asked, "Can you do a video chat if I call you right back?"

I shrugged, then realized he couldn't see that. "Yeah, of course."

He hung up. I stared at the phone, wondering how our night could get any weirder.

My phone lit up again, the video camera icon flashing ominously.

I hit the button, but instead of being treated to Gunner's intense scowl, a massive set of perfect, movie-star quality teeth filled the screen.

I was so confused. "Uh, Gunner, you need to-"

Gunner spoke, then a second voice I recognized immediately. The second voice was closer to the phone. "You're too close," Gunner was saying. "Hold the phone further away."

"Oh, thanks, dude," came the reply. The camera moved back a bit, allowing the owner of the second voice to come into full view. "Pack Man," the voice cried out. Huge, blue eyes twinkled with childlike glee. "I thought you were dead, dude!"

"Join the club," Becky mumbled.

"Hey, Cool," I replied, watching my friend, the Elastic Giraffe, smile into the camera like an influencer taking selfies. "Uh, nice to see you?"

It was going to be a long night.

To Be Continued in:
indGame: Book 2
NPCs